IN CONFIDENCE

IRÈNE NÉMIROVSKY

IN CONFIDENCE

Translated from the French by
Eoin Bates and Sandrine Brisset

RaglanBooks

RAGLAN BOOKS
2 Cheltenham Place, Portobello Bridge
Dublin 6, Ireland

http://www.raglanbooks.ie

First published in 2015

ISBN: 978-0-9574947-1-8

The publisher acknowledges the financial assistance of
Ireland Literature Exchange (translation fund), Dublin, Ireland.
www.irelandliterature.com
info@irelandliterature.com

The publisher also acknowledges the financial assistance of
the Trinity College Dublin Association and Trust
East Chapel, Trinity College, Dublin 2, Ireland
http://www.tcd.ie/alumni
alumni@tcd.ie

Contents

IN CONFIDENCE

EPILOGUE

She would come in slowly, a book in her hand, timidly tilt her head to one side, take a seat in the most deserted corner of the bar and begin to read. At that time of the day the empty bar was a sanctuary of peace. She had the frail, weary face of an old woman, a colourless complexion and lifeless eyes. When she turned the pages of the book open before her, one could see the slight tremor that shook her beautifully-shaped hands, hands which sometimes drew the attention of men, but… otherwise she was hardly a woman at all. Those who spoke of her called her 'old Alice Maynell'. She was never accompanied by anyone. Come morning, she would set off again, always alone.

Her voice was soft, muted, a little sibilant, just as refined and civilised American voices that have lost all trace of a nasal accent tend to be. 'How are you?' she would be asked. 'Oh, fine!… she would answer in English in the cheerful tone that people from her part of the world adopt when asked about their well-being, even if they feel ill or unhappy. Now and again someone would add, 'What are you reading, Mrs Maynell?'

'Oh! just trash,' she would smile. 'A detective novel, you know…'

She readily smiled a demure smile that parted her pale lips as if with some regret. Her lips, when at rest, had that bitter little contraction particular to those who speak rarely and briefly and who live in profound solitude.

A little later she lifted up her head and ordered quietly. 'Whisky…'

It was brought to her. She drank it down in one mouthful, and her hands regained their steadiness. She continued to read. Some time passed.

'Whisky…' the voice said again.

She then got up, leaving behind the book she had begun: *Scarlet and Black*, *The Idiot* or maybe *The Plays of Shakespeare*. Now at the bar, she drank silently, staring down at her glass. The shadow of her little hat, which she wore at an angle, hid her features. Only once, one Christmas night, had she drunk to the point of letting her head drop forward, and her hat had loosened and slipped off. She had red hair, not one white strand, a fiery mane full of life atop her sad, withered face. But no one looked at her. It was past midnight, and at that hour in the bar those who sensed that the outside world still existed were few and far between.

It was a small English bar, frequented almost exclusively

by English and American customers. A smell of fine aged wine and spirits that could be breathed in from the threshold, the absence of women, soft lighting inviting fatigue and drunkenness—this was what the regulars liked. They had been meeting there every evening for ten or fifteen years. Some of them who were married and settled in Paris merely passed by, had one drink and went off home. Others lived there, only leaving their seat well into the night to go back to some neighbouring hotel.

At two o'clock the intruders and the visitors retired for the night. Only the regulars—there were about ten of them—remained. All these men were at least forty years old. What they wanted was not so much to talk, but to be left in silence, not so much to drink but to sit half-asleep on an old leather seat, every hollow of which their bodies had moulded for a long time, to listen to a quiet clock ticking on the wall and, later still, to some slightly rusted, slightly worn records playing on the gramophone, tunes from the years 1920 to 1924 that brought back memories of their youth.

These customers saw the bar as their own house and the women who ran it as their true family. They brought flowers for the owner for her name day. She was attentive to them: sometimes she didn't know their names, but she knew what their favourite brand of champagne was, the dishes they liked, knew when it was time to talk to them and knew better than any wife ever could when it was better to keep quiet.

She visited them when they were sick, not sick enough for the American hospital to take them in, but on their own in their hotel rooms, their faces turned against the wall, counting the flowers on the wallpaper, healing themselves with alcohol, waiting for the fever to subside with the patience, wisdom and meekness of wounded animals. The regulars only saw one another at the bar; they never ventured to one another's homes. They were too reserved, too decent for that. It was tacitly accepted that none of them should or could ever need the others.

They didn't leave Paris when summer came. In the bar the blinds were lowered from the morning onward, and the electric lamps lit. It would have been easy to think that the night was not yet over.

When at last the summer heat died down, the door was opened and a less intense light poured in from outside. The freshly washed tiles would be slowly drying. On the threshold Mrs Maynell would appear, holding in one hand a bunch of small dark summer roses, their hearts still fragrant. She would cross the room noiselessly and sit down at her usual place.

Slowly, the long daylight faded, the cars were on their way back from the countryside, bouquets of wild flowers hanging out of the windows. One last sunbeam hit the mirror above the bar and reflected towards the ceiling a ray of sparkling light that vanished little by little. It was evening at last.

'It must be lovely by the water's edge…' Doris the little barmaid said in a sigh.

But these men, their glasses and dice cups in their hands, seemed happy.

They preferred the winter, however, especially certain

days when the rain pelted down violently, when the west wind, heavy with showers, breathed over Paris a warmish, humid, almost maritime air. There was nothing to see on the street but the occasional passer-by rushing on in the distance, head down, umbrella held forward. He might have been looked upon with pity and imagined hurrying home to a dour family, the crying of children or the whining of a wife... The shops were closing one by one. Eventually only the creamery remained open, the nearby gaslight shedding light on its basket of eggs at the door, and also a bakery in which three golden sticks of bread were left on display. Suddenly a hand grabbed them, brought them in hurriedly and closed the shutters. At the sound of the iron bar against the shutters, at that signal of a new life beginning behind the closed windows, a nocturnal, peaceful and secret life—one which contrasted with the chaos and weariness of daily life—Mrs Maynell put down her book and approached the bar, which at that time was crammed full of people. She carried herself in an excessively upright manner, with the unsteady stiffness of a drunkard, about whom it can be sensed that all their muscles and all their body and soul are strained so as to prevent a fall. Her face was tired and frightening. She sat down and was now motionless, as were her eyes, which stared at some point in the space in front of her—at the shining rim of a glass, at a light, at the copper rail that surrounded the bar—but never up at a living face.

At that moment the local wine merchant's grey cat entered. It was coming to get a piece of meat from the kitchen. Having eaten, it slinked up close to Alice Maynell.

She didn't stroke it, didn't give it anything, didn't even look at it, but let it settle itself by her side as she moved a little to the edge of the barstool to make space for it. The cat fell asleep next to her.

One day Doris, the little red-haired, milky-skinned barmaid, got engaged. The regulars all shared enthusiastically in celebrating the milestone. The young man was a soldier so the wedding ceremony would have to wait almost a year. Doris was by turns sombre and feverishly happy. One night she showed Alice Maynell the photo of her fiancé.

'Do you like him, Mrs Maynell?'

They were alone at the bar. An elderly American, Eric Braun, who sometimes spoke to Mrs Maynell, was drinking in silence, sitting at the back of the room.

'You mustn't marry that boy...' he heard Alice Maynell say quietly after she had given the photo back to Doris.

Doris made an effort to laugh.

'Really? Why not?'

Without looking up, the other woman was slowly tracing circles with her long, trembling finger on the wooden bar top. Then, with extreme care, she wrote a name, gazed at it for a moment and wiped over it with her hand.

'He has a girl's face,' she said eventually.

'No!...' Doris protested feebly. 'No he doesn't...'

The photo was of a tall, nicely built young man in a soldier's uniform, one fist on his hip, a smile on his face.

'No, Mrs Maynell... If you knew him—'

'I do know him,' Mrs Maynell said abruptly, a strange violence in her voice. 'I know that type of man, so well that I never miss one when I see him. He's well built, he's handsome. He must be a good lover. But he's a girl at heart. Have you ever looked at his mouth?... Or the shape of his eyelids?... Or his hands?... Does he have a job?'

'He's looking for one.'

'And he'll go on looking,' said Mrs Maynell, 'he'll go on... You'll be working for him, and when he comes home at night, after touching other women, you'll say to him, "Are you not tired, darling?"'

Suddenly she burst out laughing, a harsh laugh that lent her a cruel, haggard appearance.

'You'll care for him when he's sick. He'll go out with his friends to indulge in his little pleasures. You'll think, "He won't be back. He'll never come back. He's with Anne or Rose or someone else." When he does come back it's even worse... A sissy, I'm telling you... Any boy can be unfaithful to you, but there is hope. One day they get old, they get tired of hurting you. But not those boys. They enjoy the hurt they cause you even more than the pleasure they give you.'

'But they do give you some pleasure,' said Doris, lowering her eyes.

Mrs Maynell shook her head.

'In the end they don't because you end up so tired that you're no longer a woman. Even when they're dead, at last, and you say to yourself, "Now it's over. Now I'll be able to sleep in peace..." Those boys never leave you in peace. Even, she said suddenly, 'if you kill them.'

She lifted her eyelids. Her pupils were dilated and oscillating like those of a frightened cat.

'He'll never leave you alone. Never, never. I know what I'm talking about,' she said more softly.

Doris was about to answer. Mrs Maynell stopped her.

'What time is it now?'

She was staring at but not seeing the clock on the wall in front of her.

'After three...'

'It's time to go. Well, I have to go anyway...'

But she stayed where she was, turning her glass slowly between her fingers.

'There's no one left, is there?' she said.

'Only Monsieur Braun.'

'Braun? Ah! yes... Come here. Why aren't you coming?' she said suddenly, signalling to Braun to come over to her. 'Have a drink?'

Braun was tall and heavy, an American with pale features. He joined the two women. He drank standing up, both elbows on the bar.

'What will I have to drink, Doris?' Mrs Maynell said.

Without waiting for an answer, she pointed at a random bottle with the fingers of her empty glove.

'That...'

She drank a full glass of neat gin, turned to Doris, then to Braun.

'Please have a drink with me... Today is someone's birthday, a woman... a very pretty woman I knew very well… Very elegant, well loved… She'd married a good, honest boy, a musician. She was unfaithful to him. That's natural enough, isn't it? He was so enamoured of her. And what do you know, she would leave him for weeks to go gadding about with her friends… And always, when she came back after weeks of absence, the house would have to be tidy, flowers everywhere, lamplight awaiting her in case it had got dark, the supper on the table, the bath drawn, and not a cross word said… He'd be waiting. Ah, he was well trained, the poor thing!… In answer to his grievances, she'd say, "You have your music, darling. Play on and forget about me." But he ended up losing even his interest in music because you can't have two passions in your heart: one drives the other out. Eventually, this one time, he thought, "I have to free myself from this presence… Love is love, but love feeds on life, on hope… When there's no hope, love itself will gently die away…"'

She stopped talking. She was looking at her cigarette, which was no longer burning. She resumed in a different tone of voice, deep and strange.

'Well, he came home as usual, you know, relaxed, cheery, knowing that someone was waiting for him… The house was tidy… There were children, poor children… asleep upstairs… Over the years, you might have thought that they were also waiting for him to come home. They were indeed waiting, but with horror and shame,' she said in a low voice. 'There were flowers on the table, and the piano lid was up. It was the middle of the night, in the countryside. No one around, not a sound. He came in laughing, got the welcome he wanted, not a cross word said. He had a drink and something to eat while a bath was being drawn for him, then he went up the stairs. He was singing in the bath. He was singing so cheerfully that he didn't hear the door open behind him. He died of a revolver shot from behind, and so quickly that his face seemed calm and happy. A beautiful face,' she said, slowly lifting her glass to her lips.

She then realised that it was empty and set it back down on the bar top.

'What about the woman?'

She started.

'The woman? What woman?'

'The one who killed him.'

'You haven't understood anything,' Alice Maynell said sharply. 'I'm telling you that the person I'm talking about was a woman. She's dead. Her husband killed her.'

'All right! But what happened to the killer? Was he arrested?'

'No, he wasn't arrested. They thought it was a black servant who had killed her. Yes, to rob the house afterwards and run off. He ran off so well, so far away that he was never found. These people I'm telling you about weren't wealthy but they had extremely wealthy parents who covered everything up... with great prudence and decency... They couldn't have been done it better or more wisely...'

She was shaking now. She looked around her and complained to Doris: 'Where's my coat?... I can't find my coat. I'm cold.'

'You didn't have a coat with you, Madame,' Doris

answered more gently. 'Have another drink, that'll warm you up.'

She obliged without a word and, as if the last glass had galvanised her, she picked herself up and threw some money in front of her, a few banknotes that she had pulled at random from her bag. Then, with the stiff but assured walk of a blind person, she reached the door, opened it and disappeared.

The following day she was back at her usual place.

As it happened, the bar was sold some months later, all its furniture sold off in lots, and on its site a cheap bric-a-brac shop was opened.

The night before the closure was one of wild, boisterous revelries. The regulars made a great show of joyful nonchalance and light-heartedness. They remarked to one another that Paris was hardly short of similar establishments, that in the end it didn't really matter where the night was spent so long as the champagne was good and the prices were reasonable; that life itself could flow by between the four barest walls so long as you were always half drunk, and that was easy… It was a pity, obviously… Ten, fifteen years, night after night being greeted by the same seats, the same faces… the same old little traditions… Of course they would make new ones in some other place… But it would take some time… They were all so ravaged by alcohol that none of them relied much on time. Where else would they find that mysterious harmony between their worn-out backs and the handrail just at chest level, on which they could lean with such pleasure in their lethargy and drunkenness?

And that tranquil light, not murky or dim to the point of semi-darkness, not harsh or crude, revealing in their souls what should remain concealed, but a familiar light, so gentle in its humble copper lampshade?… It was strange… Nearly all of them had abandoned their families and friends and lived abroad, happy to suffer and die alone, without relatives around them, without wives. But the sense of community is so powerful that they had worked continuously to recreate around them a context, routines, almost a family. A pity, yes, it was a pity … But then again, they were sensible, rational people. They would bear their burden patiently, as they had always done.

In the morning they parted after much drinking and laughing and singing. Some of them would later meet again. But instead of enjoying one another's company, they would avoid each other from now on. They had been tolerant of one another due to their habit of meeting at the same time in the same place. Now that habit had been broken and each of them would be surprised to have been able to put up with the others for so long. They would now greet one another from a distance, with a sullen expression, but they would end up no longer recognising one another.

One day, two years later, in a bar in the Étoile district, Braun overheard two men talking about Alice Maynell. He listened.

'… In the American hospital,' one said, 'she'd been ill for a long time.'

He realised that Alice Maynell was dead. He had

reached that blissful stage of drunkenness that blunts the senses so much so that the news of the passing of one's dearest friend would only sink in through a sea of indifference, but his imagination seemed more vivid, more sensitive, honed by alcohol… In his mind's eye he could see that woman alone in a room in the American hospital, which was so white, so bright, where the smell of iodoform masked the dark taste of death. Poor Alice Maynell… She had always chosen the dimmest corner of the bar. She enjoyed the faint music, the low voices…

He continued to listen, but they were now talking about something else, so he asked them, 'Did you know Mrs Maynell? I happened to meet her. I hear she's died.'

'Yes… About two weeks ago. It's a terrible pity. She was still young…'

'Ah!' said Braun with surprise. 'Ah! no, it can't be the same woman.'

'The one we're talking about was called Alice Maynell. A great artist.'

'Really?'

'A remarkable pianist. But I don't think she ever played any concerts here.'

'Not that I know of.'

'She'd lived on the continent since her husband's death. A hideous crime. He'd been murdered in his bath by a black servant. I think she gave up music after that.'

'Ah! yes,' said Braun.

He considered for a moment asking where she had been buried so that he might take a flower to place on her grave. But he shrugged his shoulders and, smacking his lips impatiently, held out his empty glass to the barman. Their whisky wasn't any good. But he drank it anyway and forgot.

AN HONEST MAN

The men were playing tarot in a village bar. It was Easter Sunday. Every time the door opened to let in a big ruby-red faced newcomer dressed in his Sunday best, his new shoes squeaking on the slippery tiles, the cold breath of spring also entered—a rush of that pure, biting wind that blew from the Morvan—and the scent of rain-soaked lilac. Outside the windows stretched the grey street to one side, and to the other lay a small garden full of soft, dew-laden flowers; a small white plum tree was quivering beneath the sullen sky. Already, in the low houses, in the kitchens, the women were chattering away; they had come back from prayers, and the soup was cooking over the fire. They were talking very loudly so that they could be heard over the sound of the butter sizzling in the pan. The men's meal was ready. However, they were in no hurry to return home: at the Hôtel des Voyageurs some of them were playing a round that was still undecided, while others were counting their winnings; a last drop of red wine was ordered. Their elbows resting on the table, their cards thrown down before them, they sat breathing in the thick pipe smoke and slowly turning their glasses between their hard hands, the cracks of which the soil had filled like black furrows, they relished their rest. There were a few middle-class men among them— the solicitor, the tax collector and the bailiff—but the company was mostly made up of wealthy farmers and livestock dealers.

It was the time of day when the little girls from the parish youth association were coming out of the church; the old women, holding their metal cups, were making their way towards the farms. The cows were being milked; the smell filled the air. The sun appeared for a second and glimmered through the rain, through the dust of the room, forming a golden pillar above the billiard table. The bells were ringing out. Some of the most elderly and most respectable men, who didn't frequent the bars but stayed at home on Sundays or accompanied their wives to vespers, were stepping cautiously out of their homes. The retired teacher passed by, followed by the doctor, and then Monsieur Mitaine, one of the most important landlords in the area. People spoke in respectful terms of him, 'He's very comfortable… He's not badly off, that's for sure!'

He owned a large white house by the river and three handsome estates.

The solicitor had finally decided to abandon his cards but was lingering on the doorstep, his hat on his head, his belly protruding, a cigar in his mouth, happy to feel such a strong warm sunbeam on his face at the end of a rainy day. He had chubby rosy cheeks and beady black eyes that glistened like olives floating in oil. He bid Monsieur Mitaine an enthusiastic goodbye; without pausing, the latter waved and said, 'See you later, then.'

When he had left, his friends asked Maître Cénard, 'Do you have dealings with Monsieur Mitaine?'

The solicitor's big coral lips smiled reticently so as to signal that he didn't wish to say either way, then he pouted to remind them that he was bound by professional secrecy. The men didn't press him. They talked about the following day's fair. Meanwhile, Monsieur Mitaine was walking on, responding solemnly to greetings. He was old and thin, dressed entirely in grey, and had a pale honest face with a big pointed, shiny nose; he looked upon people with a kindly gaze and an air of gentleness, naivety and a barely noticeable reserve, the retiring modesty particular to certain solitary old men. Elderly, unhappy and ill men seem to have been soaked either in an acid that corrodes their skin and deeply furrows their features or in a milk bath that turns their flesh soft and flabby like a fish cooked in cream. Old Monsieur Mitaine was of the second kind. He walked slowly; when spoken to, he coughed a little behind his filoselle-gloved hand before answering; his voice was weak but distinct. He was well-respected in the area. It was said of him, 'He's an honourable man. He gives everyone due credit.' He was a 'foreigner'. He was the son of a lacemaker from Douai; he had spent half his life there, leaving after the Great War. His inheritance had made him rich; he had been living in the village for twenty years; before they came into his possession, his house and estates had belonged to one of his aunts, who, unlike him, was a native of the region. In spite of everything, it had taken five or six years for people to get used to him, and in the meantime he had found that it was to his own advantage to be kept at a distance and left alone. When the tacit exclusion that weighs over all newcomers had dissipated, he declined invitations and made no friends. But he wasn't resented for this. Quite the contrary. To prefer to stay at home to playing cards at the young doctor's house or hunting with the mayor was seen as a mark of serious-mindedness, a character trait that commanded respect. Monsieur Mitaine lived with an old lady, his sister, who had never married. He had long been a widower. His only son had settled in Dijon several years previously. A boarder in a school in Nevers, then a student in Paris, he was barely known to the people of the village. It was said that his father had initially wanted to buy him a solicitor's office in the neighbouring town but had later changed his mind. 'Dijon's more prestigious, you see,' people remarked, 'and Monsieur Mitaine wanted the best for his son.'

Maître Cénard felt a slight sense of curiosity as he entered the old man's house, which he had never been in before. The doctor had frequently been called to Mitaine's house over the past while; the old man seemed enfeebled and unwell. Maître Cénard believed it was about his will and mentally calculated the inheritance he would have to look after in the not-too-distant future. He assessed at a glance the austere grey building dating back to the First Empire and the large garden sheltered by its high walls. Monsieur Mitaine lived in the village itself but offered only the view of his closed shutters and bolted door to passers-by: that part of his residence was unoccupied and he refused to let it to anyone. He shared the ground floor and its large icy rooms with his sister. Maître Cénard knocked on a door chosen at random and found himself in the vast kitchen; old Mademoiselle Mitaine was by herself, keeping warm by the stove. She was a frail, dignified person with wavy white hair parted in the middle and drawn back over her ears. Like her brother, she had an air of shy ingenuousness, albeit coloured by a hint of bitterness, so that she resembled an old cat nestling into a corner for fear of the cold and seemingly thinking, 'These clumsy fools are going to step on my paws again. These things only happen to me.' She told Maître Cénard that her brother had nodded off upon getting back home and that she didn't dare wake him because he suffered from very painful palpitations when his sleep was suddenly interrupted. She assured him, however, that she would hear him calling soon as his short naps never lasted longer than fifteen or thirty minutes. She pointed to the clock with her knitting needle.

'Five minutes, Maître Cénard.' She sighed. 'I find he's very low, very tired. He's got it into his head that he doesn't have much longer left. He wants to consult you about his will.'

'That's prudent of him,' Maître Cénard said.

Just then he considered that his words weren't altogether... He blushed and gave a little cough.

'It's never killed anyone,' he continued in an encouraging tone. 'Only last month I was called out to Nevers, to a clinic where a sick man wanted to make his will. It proved a miracle: he recovered almost instantly. Your brother has only one child, isn't that so?'

'An only son,' Mademoiselle Mitaine said.

She raised her handkerchief to her eyes and suddenly began to cry.

Not knowing what stance to take, the solicitor forced an embarrassed little laugh and instantly blushed even more.

'He wants,' said Mademoiselle Mitaine, wiping away her tears, 'to withhold part of his estate from him and leave the poor child only what the law forbids him to give away to others.'

'His legal share,' the solicitor murmured mechanically.

'Yes, and to bequeath the rest to me.'

'He's very fond of you.'

'It's obviously a great testament to how fond he is of me, and as our poor father used to say, never look a gift-horse in the mouth, but on the other hand, what will my nephew think? He'll think I'm a schemer. He'll have a falling-out with me. He's so uncompromising! He adores his father. He's already accusing me of having added fuel to the fire after that sorry business of the strongbox. Anyway, Maître Cénard, it's sad, it's so sad. That my brother might leave me some souvenir, the enjoyment of this house, for instance, or some of the furniture, that's all I'm asking, but enough is enough. At my age you don't need much. I have the appetite of a bird: a cup of milk is dinner enough for me. What I need is a bit of affection,' she murmured, and the tears she had dried began to flow again.

'You have no family besides your nephew?'

'No, no, nobody. My brother and I were left with no mother at a very young age. As for our father, I don't mean to speak ill of the dead, but he was difficult, oh, very difficult, and if my brother hadn't taken me in… I became attached to my nephew as to a son. His aunt Héloïse… He used to love me so much, Maître Cénard, and now here I am robbing him of his due… Now of all times, when he's so unhappy: he's married a penniless woman, who's always sick, and he has two little children.'

'He'll inherit from you later; you'll be able to come to his aid as soon as you take possession of your legacy.'

The old lady leaned in towards Maître Cénard and said in his ear, 'He wants me to sell everything against life annuity.'

'We'll see, we'll see,' the solicitor said. 'Don't you worry yet, Mademoiselle. Monsieur Mitaine is elderly, he's tired, but he's not going to die tomorrow, and a will can be revoked. I gather his son upset him, did he? With his marriage, perhaps?'

'No, no, it's this strongbox business.'

'Ah! The strongbox—'

'Yes. 200,000 francs disappeared from my brother's box, and he accused poor little Gérard. But the boy wasn't alone in the house. There was his friend, who had been spending his holidays here with us and who was living a life… with a nasty woman from Paris, from what I've been told, someone who's been involved in the theatre. He managed to disappear two weeks later, the wicked man! My nephew only made one mistake: he got along a little too well with those two: little trips to Dijon and Nevers, afternoon drinks together, the picture house in town on Saturdays! But in the end the young thing got tired of it! He was twenty-two. As far as I'm concerned, it's the Parisian who stole the money. The boy is innocent. But his father has never believed him. He's mortally offended the young thing by calling him a thief, and that's what's eating away at my poor brother, that's what's killing him. That's his illness. Gérard meant everything in the world to him. And now he's disinheriting him.'

'It's a misunderstanding. It's most regrettable,' the solicitor said.

The gentle heat of the stove and the little glasses of marc he had drunk at the Hôtel des Voyageurs were making him pleasantly numb.

Maître Cénard, in a confused reverie, listened to the old lady continue her account, or rather start it again, hardly changing any of the words. Her weak and monotonous little voice flowed so softly that after a few minutes he stopped hearing it. On the wall a large clock was ticking: it chimed the half hour after rumbling, chugging and groaning.

'Héloïse…' Monsieur Mitaine called from behind the door. 'Is Maître Cénard there?'

The solicitor went in to his client. Monsieur Mitaine was resting on his bed but got up to meet his visitor. He apologised for having disturbed him on a holiday but he said he wanted to consult him about a legal document that he wished to draw up as soon as possible.

'Early next week,' he said. 'It's urgent, most urgent. It's my will.'

'Oh! It's not that urgent,' Maître Cénard protested with a smile.

Dimples hollowed his big hairy cheeks when he smiled.

'You're not there yet.'

It was a sentence he always used in these circumstances, even when the person who had called for him was visibly in the throes of death upon his arrival. Monsieur Mitaine didn't respond. Reaching for a piece of paper, he took it and ran his trembling hands over it to smooth it out gently with his trembling hands.

'You can let me know if it's put in the appropriate legal terms. I'm only giving you the substance of it: "This is my last will and testament. Made this Easter Sunday 1938. I, the undersigned, being of sound mind and body…"'

'May I—'

'Yes, yes, just a moment,' said Monsieur Mitaine, who appeared suddenly overwhelmed with feverish haste and anxiety. 'I'm only giving you the substance of it. "I, the undersigned... declare that I wish to bequeath to my son Gérard Mitaine, residing in Dijon, 2, rue Charrue, only the share of my estate which the law prohibits me from distributing in accordance with my wishes, this because my son Gérard has gravely failed me." Treated by me with great affection—with immeasurable affection,' Monsieur Mitaine said more quietly as he dropped the piece of paper he was holding and looked up at the solicitor with eyes reddened by sleeplessness, fever or tears, 'with a leniency for which I reproach myself at times, he has repaid me with nothing but odious ingratitude. He has robbed me. He took advantage of a short trip I had to take to the capital— and this to undergo a life-threatening operation—he took advantage of my having foolishly left him with the key to my strongbox to open it and rob me of the 200,000 francs in banknotes inside. I didn't deserve this. I really didn't deserve this. I was only ever a good example to him. I never treated him harshly or even strictly. He never wanted for anything, neither for his education nor his leisure. Why has he done this? Why?'

He was no longer talking to Maître Cénard: he seemed to be repeating a question formulated a long time ago in the hidden depths of his heart and to which he had never found any answer.

'The influence of bad company, probably,' said the solicitor, embarrassed. 'But was there not... Did I not hear that there was a stranger in the house at the time of the theft?'

'No, no, it could only have been my son, I'm afraid. I'm certain of it.'

'You have evidence then?'

'A stranger would have been afraid to rob me. But he knew he wasn't risking anything since the law doesn't recognise theft between parents and children.'

'But that's not evidence, Monsieur Mitaine!'

'A father never makes mistakes. There are certain words, looks, blushes that are worse than a confession, Maître Cénard. My poor sister is telling me that Gérard is innocent, but only to comfort me, like you.'

'Oh, me,' Maître Cénard said with a guarded pout, signalling with a gesture of his big arms that he had no opinion on the matter. 'But,' he continued after a moment's reflection, 'why do you want to specify the… the nature of the disagreement between you and your son? The will itself is explicit. He'll see clearly that he's upset you when he learns that part of his inheritance has been withheld from him.'

'No, no, I want to put it in black and white. I don't want his sons to judge me later the way others have—'

He paused.

'He'll raise my grandchildren against me.'

'You're putting them at a disadvantage too.'

'I've never seen them! I don't know them. My son got married without telling me. I don't have any affection for those little ones, who, by the way, will grow up to be just like Gérard. It's a natural law, you see. I see it now, it's the law of God. Honour thy father and thy mother. I can see Gérard's children already!' the old man suddenly exclaimed in a strange, barely audible voice as a rush of blood rose to his pale cheeks. 'I can see them already in twenty years' time, creeping into their father's house, opening the cabinets, rummaging through his boxes, robbing him, helping themselves, spending their inheritance before their father has even died! From one generation to the next, nothing changes, everything repeats itself.'

He fell into a deep reverie.

'Please, Maître Cénard,' he concluded briefly, 'take this little note. Examine it! Think about it and draw up the document so that everything is done by the end of this week. I'm very tired. I'll rest more easily when all the loose ends have been tied up.'

'It can be done as early as Tuesday, if you like.'

They set a date. Maître Cénard left. The visit had depressed him and he didn't know why. He stopped by the Hôtel des Voyageurs once again before going home and drank two large glasses of Beaujolais. Slowly he began to smile at life again. He would have pike for dinner; he had a good cook.

Meanwhile, Monsieur Mitaine had carefully tidied the will away in a drawer of his table. He was an orderly man. His papers were sorted into coloured folders and labelled: Taxes, Property, Personal Documents. This last folder contained photographs of Gérard and his first composition, 'Describe a Spring Day'. The old man went through the photos one by one: Gérard at eighteen, in Paris, with a little blonde moustache, the colour of a chick's down, which he had had shaved off the following year; Gérard at twelve at the time of his first communion; Gérard at five, in trousers too long for him and with tightly cropped hair, the sad, unkempt look of a motherless child: the poor woman had just died. It was 1918. They were still living in Douai at the time. He had done everything in the world to look after his little one and make him happy regardless, but some thanks he had got since then! Men remember the past through moments, through surges of melancholy that soon dissipate, to be replaced by the hustle and bustle and worries of everyday life. But at Monsieur Mitaine's age the past and life itself are one and the same. It occurred to him constantly that however sad or bitter the past may have been at times, it was better than the present: that loneliness, the sound of the clock in the big kitchen, the clicking of Héloïse's knitting needles, the quiet crackling of the fire in the stove.

Monsieur Mitaine had been born and raised in Douai. His father was a severe, avaricious and morally dissolute man. As far back as his childhood days, Joseph Mitaine had instinctively hated his father, who beat him, was unfaithful to his wife with a servant and various factory workers, who was rude, vain and dishonest. As a child he had shown himself to be good, sensitive, scrupulous and polite. In school he had been a model student, a teacher's pet, and even now, at seventy-four years of age, he could still occasionally remember with a shiver of distress the way his schoolmates had made him pay for his good behaviour. Poor Joseph had never been happy! He bowed his head, overwhelmed with the deep melancholy of old age: the realisation that life has come to an irrevocable end and hasn't been kind. He had been made fun of because he was shy, because he hated in equal measure hitting others and being hit, because he didn't swear and refused to smoke in secret. He had known all the pleasures reserved for honest people in the world—peace of mind, self-esteem and esteem from others, yes, all those pleasures… As for everything else… He had been abused when he was a child; he had been deceived and robbed when he became a man. Made to marry very young by his father, he was cuckolded ten months later. His wife had run away with an officer. He hadn't wanted to work with his father; he had a small ribbon factory; his business wasn't doing well. He had been frugal, upstanding, discreet, obliging, but he had no luck. Out of pride, he had refused to ask his father for any help; he hadn't allowed himself to hope for his father's death, but every night he had dreamt that he was told of his passing, that he was called to the solicitor's and received his inheritance. At times the dream brought with it grotesque or indecent details that tormented Monsieur Mitaine upon awaking. 'As Maistre put it,' he would say to himself with sadness and confusion, "I don't know what goes on in the mind of a rascal, but I do know what goes on in the mind of an honest man, and it's awful!"'

When his wife died, Monsieur Mitaine had hesitated for a long time before remarrying: he wanted a family, a son, but his first experience had made him timid. He had a pleasant face but thought he was ugly; he was intelligent, cultured, but any country bumpkin could make him feel shy. 'I'd want a rich woman with a good reputation in the area, from a good background, someone who would stop me from acting the fool, as I do, since I'm the poor one in the family,' he sometimes thought after an evening spent in a drawing room in Douai, without him having so much as opened his mouth, and having behaved in so self-effacing a manner, so lost in his little corner, that the young lady of the house had forgotten to offer him some coffee. Eventually, at the age of forty-eight, he married a penniless orphan, a very young little teacher who had just come to Douai. How they had loved each other! Gérard had inherited her pretty face, her deep pale eyes. Old Monsieur Mitaine, alone in his room, stared with melancholy at the blooming fruit trees in his garden, thinking of his house in Douai, of his young wife, now twenty years dead, of his son whose birth he had not dared hope for, who had been born to him almost in his old age, of those happy days. For he had been happy for two or three years. His marriage, a folly in other people's eyes, had raised him up in his own view. Certain that he was loved, he no longer sought sympathy in others, and now they offered it to him unreservedly, for the only thing that comes easily is the very thing you no longer want. He wasn't rich: he could hardly make ends meet, but Madame Mitaine was a good housewife; their tastes were, to his mind as to hers, modest; he was content with his lot. He was even indifferent to the news that late in life his father had kept a mistress in his house and that he was making arrangements, even in his own lifetime, to leave his entire estate to her in order to dispossess his legitimate heirs, Joseph and Héloïse, whom he had never been able to tolerate. Indeed none of this truly mattered to him. He knew he was honest and reasonable. His life would pass by without event, but his son would later think of him affectionately and with pride. Even now his fellow countrymen respected him, alluded to him as a model of integrity and relied on him to resolve their disagreements, those concerning not money, but honour.

Then came the Great War. Monsieur Mitaine was fifty. His health was fragile. He wanted to enlist. He was turned down. He stayed in Douai, and that was the beginning of his troubles. As early as the first weeks of the war he was ruined. No one was buying ribbons any more. The factory gates shut until better times. At the beginning of 1916 the Mitaines found themselves in an almost desperate situation. 'A drowning man,' the old man thought of that sorry past, 'a man swimming peacefully on a fine summer day who starts sinking, suddenly caught up in the storm, cries out in vain, struggles and disappears.' In the small apartment where he had found refuge with his loved ones, he was cold and hungry. He had remained discreet in his poverty; if he asked for help, it was in such a detached, humble tone that it was easier to say no to him than to anyone else. He wouldn't accept any money: what he wanted was work, but there was none for him. He was very well received when he came looking for favours. 'My poor friend,' people would sigh, 'we're all miserable. The war...' But there are gradations of misery: his former friends didn't realise this, and he was very slowly reaching the last point on the scale, after which there is only death.

He remembered those increasingly paltry meals, after which, getting up from the table, he would think, 'How many more times will we be able to eat?' He remembered those nights when, lying beside his wife, both of them awake in the dark, each pretended to be asleep so that the other might at least be at peace and not suffer. At times a kind of stupor would come over him: 'My God... this is unbelievable. Something has to save me... This is crazy. I've never hurt anyone, I don't deserve this...' Then he stopped thinking 'I'. He saw himself as lost, having reached the end of his life, and as for his wife, he was abandoning her to her own fate, but there was still Gérard. It was around that time that his wife took ill and he had to look after Gérard, wash him, dress him, feed him. In clumsily working through these women's chores, he grew even closer to the little boy, and his fatherly love became compounded with something corporeal, pitiable and tender that sometimes gnawed at his heart. Indeed he felt it almost physically. He awoke at night to feel something in his chest hurting him, as if some creature had been feeding on his flesh from the inside. One day, finally... It was a winter day, a cold day, it was the war. He left his house and went to his father's. He didn't know why he was going there. His father and his mistress had left Douai in a hurry within the first days of the war and had never been able to return. He had looked at the closed shutters and the grey walls. 'If I had just a small share of what's in there…' he had thought sadly. The silverware alone was worth… What was it worth? He had shuddered. It belonged to his father. He could have asked him for his help (and he could imagine the greedy, callous old man's blunt refusal), but to creep into his house without his permission, to make off with… Theft. It was theft. To some other, less scrupulous conscience than his own, such an act might have seemed acceptable, excusable—who knows?—but to him… In any case, the door was locked. He had approached it and had absent-mindedly rang the bell. He had heard the sound it made, sharp and prolonged, and suddenly the door had opened. A woman appeared. It was one of his father's former cooks. She lived in the house next door, held the keys and sometimes came to do the housework.

'Ah, is that you, my dear Eugénie?' Monsieur Mitaine had said, his voice soft, friendly and cheerful. 'If I'd known earlier that you had the keys… I've left some of my belongings upstairs. Yes, in the silverware cabinet, it's been hiding there for years, a little silver cup I'd like to give to my child.'

He had sold the cup two weeks previously.

'Well, come upstairs then, Monsieur Joseph!'

She went along with him, jingling the keys.

'Oh, there's no need. I'll go up by myself.'

'Ah! This is to open the shutters.'

She ushered him into the butler's pantry and opened the louvred shutters and the window.

'Leave me with the keys then. I'll bring them back to you when I come down,' he had said with a little laugh.

'Certainly, Monsieur Joseph. There's a lot of dust, but I only come here once a week to do a quick run through the place. Everything's been abandoned. Oh well, at least we can be glad we haven't had any bombings in this part of town.'

'Yes, isn't that so? We haven't suffered too much up to now,' Monsieur Mitaine had said.

Once on his own, with extraordinary agility and precise, nimble movements unknown to himself, he searched through the drawers systematically. First the spoons: those were the heaviest. He had pushed aside the ivory-handled knives. He had bundled the forks together and shoved them into his jacket pocket. His heart had begun to race as he had opened a small case and saw two gold frames in it. His pockets were full: he had taken an empty hatbox that was lying nearby, had filled it with the most disparate items, then had looked around to see what remained: dresses left behind in the wardrobes by his father's mistress, furs, offcuts of fabric that could be used to dress Gérard. He had nothing; the smallest thing was of great value to him. He had seen a new pair of shoes in a cupboard. He had grabbed them.

'Has Monsieur found what he was looking for?' the cook suddenly said behind him.

He had a few francs left, which were meant to pay for the following day's dinner. He didn't hesitate.

'Here, my dear Eugénie... No, I insist, take it! And I'll tell you what, I'll probably be back tomorrow. It's very strange, there are many more of my things here than I'd thought.'

They looked at each other in silence for a moment. She knew he was lying. She was aware that he had fallen out with his father and that he hadn't stepped foot in the house in ten years. She probably thought, 'Ah well! By the time the old man comes back!' Between the north and the rest of France the war had raised a barrier of flames, of death. She realised that he would give her a little money each time. She smiled.

'Well, let Monsieur come back whenever he pleases.'

He might not have come back, had the two frames really been made of gold, as he had believed. But they were worthless. The disappointment he had felt as a result was such that he had returned to his father's house the very next day with an empty suitcase, in which he had concealed his spoils on the way out. He was back three days later with a wheelbarrow to take away piles of sheets, towels and all the undergarments belonging to his father's mistress. He had kept six beautiful blouses for his wife and sold the rest. Little by little he removed almost all the furnishings. He was living well now. His apartment was small but had beautiful carpets, ornaments and the big silk curtains that his father's mistress had bought in Lyon; it began to look pleasant. The Mitaines were saved at last. The only thing that troubled him was his conscience. He didn't feel any regret, but that was only natural: all in all, according to every man-made and God-given law, his father's fortune ought to have been his. What's more, he had been driven to act as he did by necessity. No, what surprised him was the extraordinary pleasure he had derived from the expedition. It wasn't even a vengeful pleasure: he bore no grudges, and he felt so morally superior to his father that he could scarcely be annoyed with him. No! As a celibate who eventually lies with a woman comes to know exquisite and unsuspected pleasures in debauchery, as a temperate man who, having drunk excessively one night, learns to appreciate and compare fine wines, similarly, Monsieur Mitaine was savouring deceit, hypocrisy and theft; profound, intense sensations came over him when he fled from his father's house at nightfall, when he felt in his pocket something that he had made off with (a snuffbox, a watch, a ring left in a writing desk), when he estimated its value and waited to be back home to examine what he had taken under a better light. Everything—a greeting from a friend encountered on the streets of Douai as he was hurrying along, clutching some stolen silver platter against his heart, the shady dealings required to relieve himself of his hauls, the cook's knowing glance—everything amused him, excited him and gave his life a sweet charm that had previously been lacking. His wife was ill. She had reached that stage of tuberculosis when the outside world becomes as unreal as a dream. She had no interest in the source of their newfound wealth; she had never questioned her husband; she was dying peacefully. 'Yes, at least she died peacefully,' Monsieur Mitaine had thought, and he remembered the visits he had paid to his father's house to get some clothes, linen, a comfortable dressing gown, a pair of slippers for himself. In the occupied, war-besieged city where the bare necessities were nowhere to be found, Monsieur Mitaine had been alone in being in possession of luxuries.

Once the war was over, he had learned that his father had died so suddenly that he hadn't had the time to leave anything to his mistress. Monsieur Mitaine was rich. Several months later he lost his wife. He was never happy again, but he was satisfied materially. Inheritances—some of which he hadn't even expected—had made him rich. He left Douai with Gérard as soon as he could and, having taken in Héloïse, who had spent the four years of the war in southern France, he settled in the village where he still was now. He rarely gave a thought to this past experience but realised that it had kneaded his soul like dough. He was changed, enriched by a bitter experience. He had known a moral loneliness so dark and so harsh that it would never be cleared from his memory. In his sense of justice, and later in his charity, in his benevolence there was always a slight sour aftertaste, a hint of reproach: 'I never had such luck,' he thought whenever he helped the poor. Nothing came of it; just as a slow-acting toxin poisons the body little by little and only reveals its lethal effects after several months, or sometimes several years, so Monsieur Mitaine's actions, although justified a thousand times in his own eyes, corrupted his soul. He had been the most trusting of men; now he was suspicious of his neighbour's every intention. 'If I've done it,' he thought, 'why not others?'

One should never look too deeply into one's heart: it's disturbing and frightening. Monsieur Mitaine, at least, had been disturbed and frightened by it. All his interactions with his son had been warped by that memory. 'He's telling me the truth,' he thought, when his son was denying some schoolboy error. 'Why would he lie? True, but on the other hand, why would he not? I've told my share of lies!' He remembered the provincial house with its huge pieces of furniture covered with dust sheets, the silverware cabinet, the key in the old cook's hand, the ambivalent look in her eyes, her smile. 'What if it weren't my father's house but someone else's, a stranger's, and if I had found myself in the same situation? What would have held me back from stealing? Fear of the law, nothing else. So if I've done it, why not him?' Tonight, when his sister Héloïse came timidly into his room, imploring him once again with tears in her eyes to think it over and not accuse Gérard, he still answered, 'My poor dear, you don't know men.'

He felt so weak that he refused to come out of his room for supper. Héloïse served him his food on a tray at his bedside; he took small, reluctant bites. The cheerful din of the village reached them through the thick walls. After such a rainy day, the evening was pleasant. It was nearly dark, but young men and women were still walking along the road, the boys on one side, the girls on the other, in groups, and their laughter and jokes became interwoven in the air, which had suddenly grown milder. The wind had died down. The cats were

45

scurrying around the garden, leaping nimbly over the freshly seeded flower beds.

'Would you not forgive Gérard?' Héloïse murmured.

He shook his head violently. No, he wouldn't forgive him: he had loved him too much. His own father had deserved to be robbed, but not him. And that someone else might be the guilty party didn't enter into his mind. Perhaps his strictness with his son, the severity that was killing him, was a form of punishment that he was inflicting on himself. Maybe... This thought came to Monsieur Mitaine's tired soul, and sometimes touched it like a bird brushing the tip of its wing against a closed window, then drifted away. He felt very old, very unwell and very sad.

He took ill a few days after signing the will. He had taken too much of a narcotic prescribed by the doctor, who found himself forever at his beside. It was a mistake, of course. An earnest, wealthy old man wouldn't commit suicide. His death was expected from one moment to the next.

As usual, Maître Cénard was spending the evening at the Hôtel des Voyageurs when a car came to a halt in front of the door. A young man carrying a suitcase got out.

'Why, that's Mitaine's son,' the chambermaid said with astonishment.

Everyone was surprised to see him coming in. Was he not staying with his father then? He asked for a room.

'I was embarrassed for him,' the manageress said later. 'I'd been told that his father didn't want to see him but I didn't believe it. They say the old man's forbidden Mademoiselle Héloïse to let his son know when he feels the end coming on. Yes, I found it very odd altogether when he told me he'd be spending the night here.'

At the time she had hesitated before mentioning his father.

'We weren't expecting you so soon, Monsieur…' she eventually sighed. 'It's terribly sad…'

When Hortense, the chambermaid, came up to make the bed and slip the hot water bottle between the covers, she had found Gérard Mitaine standing at the window. He hadn't even taken off his overcoat or unpacked his suitcase. He had thrown his gloves on the table and was looking out the window at his father's house, of which only the upstairs was visible.

'Oh! He looks so sad,' Hortense said after coming down to the kitchen.

Maître Cénard smiled with pity and with the kind of involuntary wryness one feels towards a stranger whose most intimate secrets chance has revealed to you. So that slim young dark-haired man, who seemed so respectable, had rummaged around in his father's box! Unless he was taking the blame for someone else? He patted his big belly with a little grimace of pleasure.

'We come across all sorts in our trade,' he thought once more.

Meanwhile, Gérard, his door locked, let tears roll down his face. His aunt had sent somebody to call for him the day before, strongly advising that he not try to see the old man. 'Your father doesn't want to see you. He says he wants to die alone, as he's lived. If he changes his mind at the last moment, I'll let you know,' his aunt had said, 'and if he dies, well, you'll know straight away: I'll turn off the light in the upstairs bedroom.'

The lamp, visible through the shutters, was still glowing.

'Poor father,' Gérard said softly.

He was crying about both the old man and himself. He was innocent. His friend's mistress had made him drink one night and, having made off with the key to the strongbox, had stolen the money that was in it. But his father had never believed him.

It was strange: Gérard resented him, he was hurt, but the fact that his father had remained so faithful to his principles filled him with a sort of bitter admiration. A son can forgive his father anything if he stays true to the image he has projected of himself. In Gérard's eyes, old Monsieur Mitaine was honour personified. He almost understood him, and that night he forgave him his severity.

He waited for quite some time, hoping in vain for a call. Suddenly the light went out.

LUNCH IN SEPTEMBER

Thérèse Dallas paused for a moment, looked at the reflection of her face in the narrow mirror fitted between two shopfronts, sighed and quickly crossed the street. That September morning bore the heat of high summer; beneath the blazing sun her make-up was gently melting on her tired skin. On her cheeks, which had not lost their clean contours but had nonetheless grown flabby and swollen by the onset of her forties, the powder and blusher formed a smooth, creamy coating like beautiful fine porcelain, but around the deeply sunken corners of her eyes and mouth the first cracks were appearing.

'Forty tomorrow...' Thérèse thought.

She picked up her pace. There were few passers-by; September was only beginning. The trees already bore pink autumn leaves, but the sun was strong, the air stifling. Women selling fruit and vegetables were pushing their little handcarts along the pavement, and the wilted flowers were drooping out of narrow green sheet-metal vases. You could nonetheless tell it was autumn because of the cascades of muscat grapes and pears, which were already heavy and beautiful, their yellow curves powdered in pink.

Thérèse crossed the threshold of the little English bar to which the Dallases had been coming for many years. From a van parked at the door a young red-haired girl was unloading long golden sticks of bread.

'Is Monsieur Dallas not with you?' she asked, smiling.

'He left this morning, May,' Thérèse said.

She went in. As usual the little dark room was suffused with a luscious but barely noticeable aroma of fine aged wine and spirits. A bluish mist covered the mirrors like the light dust found on the dark skins of plums. It was a little English bar visited by hardly anyone but foreigners from North America and England, mainly middle-aged men and women who drank and ate in silence and, despite often meeting there twice in the one day, exchanged only brief, silent greetings from a distance. Fried eggs with bacon, rare roasts served the English way, on a plate of tender lentils, and golden kippers were the order of the day.

In the old days this was the secret place where Thérèse and François Dallas used to meet around the time they got engaged, some twenty years ago. But Thérèse turned her mind away from those bygone days... Saccharine memories can sour over the years and form in the soul a kind of mawkish sediment like the dregs left by a sugared wine at the bottom of a glass.

These days they met there once or twice a week at six o'clock. François's office was around the corner. Thérèse congratulated herself on having made it there that morning, on having avoided a lonely lunch in the summer apartment that was strewn with dust sheets and saturated with the smell of Fly-tox. She had been feeling weary over the past few weeks for no reason. The fresh air and the solitude of the bar had a relaxing effect on her. She looked benevolently at the English pictures of horses and hunters that covered the pale walls.

The orange blind was drawn halfway down, it filtered through a whole host of sunbeams that seemed to be rising up from the ground, from the burning pavement, and which were reflected in a large mirror suspended above the bar and glittering in the shade like a silver shield.

The red-haired girl approached Thérèse.

'Are you not going to have your lunch now, Madame?'

'At noon.'

'Would you like something to drink while you're waiting?'

'An orange juice,' Thérèse said.

Doris, May's mother—the bar was managed by women—came to serve her.

'Madame Dallas,' she said with a smile, 'one of our longest-standing customers, whom we hadn't seen in quite a while, came back yesterday. One of your old friends,' she added after a moment's reflection. 'What a pity Monsieur Dallas isn't here!'

'Who was it?'

'Monsieur Cazeneuve.'

'Raymond Cazeneuve!' Thérèse murmured with surprise and a sudden deep, confused melancholy. 'Oh, my God, that's going back a while!'

She was alone. She wrapped her warm hands around the ice-cold glass. Raymond... In a flash she saw his face again and she looked down immediately and began to tidy mechanically the packages she had placed beside her on the bench alongside a bouquet of black-hearted marigolds. All of a sudden she recalled that silk ribbon that didn't seem broad enough; she unwrapped the paper, pulled one end of the ribbon, gazed at it without seeing it, forced once more her thoughts to the tea towels, which were lovely but so expensive... to the Marseille soap that hadn't been delivered the day before... 'The shopping, the maids, money... life is tedious. My God, it's extraordinary how tedious a life 'on the go' can be... Why? Oh!' she answered herself in her head—'nuisances, illnesses, worries, money—money most of all... and all the rest... And yet before? Before?...'

All of a sudden she looked at the little bar as if she were searching the shade for the image of a twenty-year-old Thérèse Dallas and a young François... In those days... All at once she remembered; in her innermost self she rediscovered forgotten memories... In those days an old fortune teller in a black satin dress and a feathered hat used to come there… In a jet-embroidered reticule a blackened deck of tarot cards, the like of which Thérèse had never seen since… In those days an old black man who had since died or gone away, absent for years, used to come to play music in the evening. He would sit in that corner, on the right… He had a face more brownish than black, like coffee diluted in water, rather long silver hair and a little white moustache. He would make strange plaintive sounds, like the humming of a wasp, with his banjo—'was it a banjo or a guitar?' She could still see him. He would tilt his head to one side, whistling and tapping out the beat with his foot in creaking patent leather shoes.

Back then the little English bar wasn't quiet as it was now. It was the Twenties… the post-war years… A turbulent memory, burning with melancholy, lingered in the depths of her soul. Funny… she could see it all over again, even the horse chestnuts in bloom on the nearby avenue on the way home at daybreak, between François and… It was strange… everything except François's face when he was younger… In her memory François's ageing face appeared like a mask over his features as a twenty-year-old; charming François, whom she loved with all her heart, but… She sighed. 'I'd sooner die than see him come up against worry, sadness or an enemy,' she thought fervently, 'I'd sooner die…' But… his lumbago, his stomach aches, his short naps after lunch… or even that twitch, the tautness in his upper lip, his off-key voice singing the same tune every morning in the bath… François, in the old days,

with his ardent young face turned up towards her…
Ah well, that's how it goes… Every woman, every
marriage is the same. Although she had closed her eyes,
scrunched up her eyelids, searched for and at last found
once again François's face as a young man, it now only
stirred in her a sense of gratitude and melancholy. Love…
'That's how it goes,' she pondered again, 'what can you
do.' She watched the small silver bubbles forming on
the surface of her glass and drank distractedly. In those
days François was not the only one in her life… That
too, how… strange it was… To be so madly in love
with a man but not to think of him as the only one to
please… To dress up, to make up one's face to please
two men, to smile, tilt one's head to the side, flash one's
gleaming teeth and eyes, all to please two men… First
François, then Raymond Cazeneuve… Ah, Raymond!
She didn't need to search her memory for long to see
his thin Béarnais face, his hollow temples and his dark
mocking eyes emerge from the deep recesses of the past.
Being François's best friend at the time, naturally he
had never said a word or made any gesture… She shook
her head with a sad little sardonic smile, which she
quickly suppressed. 'That hat looks nice on you tonight,
Thérèse… You look particularly beautiful tonight…'
Words of love… As for her? It lasted two years, during
which time, as they say, 'nothing happened'. And then
he left… Nothing… When she wanted to seize gestures,
words, smiles scattered over the depths of the past, there
was nothing left but idle talk that might as well have been
spoken out of an automatic gallantry, the kind of male

flirtatiousness that is a thousand times more perverse and deeper than a woman's... Nothing... 'What about me? Is it possible that I loved him?... Loved... Love can't be compared with the feeling I had, that I still have for François...' But you don't reach forty without realising that there are many kinds of love. 'To love... I don't know... I've thought of him, I was obsessed with him... I used to dream of him the whole night through, that he loved me, that he held me in his arms... It's funny...' She started and looked nervously at the doorway with a sense of shame and dread. As in the old days... The days when she used to wait for François in this very place... 'Our love,' she thought. 'It wasn't so quiet, so steady at the start... Life isn't easy.' She used to wait like this, and every time the door opened her short-sighted eyes believed they could make out François's clothes and his face in the figure of the stranger entering, and her heart began to race ('my God, so daft!'), and when at last he appeared, that profound peace that filled her heart...

'The past,' she whispered.

She sighed. In later years she had waited for Raymond Cazeneuve in the same way. When marriage, ownership of the man she loved, had absorbed that dread, that fever, she had also waited, sitting by her husband's side, for Raymond's face, his footsteps... 'It's funny, I've always had a thirst for worry...'

She raised her head. He had just come in. She recognised him at once after the first little jolt of surprise, of disappointment. Older, heavier... But almost at once the slightly puffy face of the forty-five-year-old man who stood before her, his grey hair thinning around his temples, his mouth thin and tired revealed other features...

She held her hand out to him. He seemed neither surprised nor moved to see her, but a kind of vague melancholy softened his gaze.

'Doris told me that you still come here. I'm glad to see you again.'

'Me too,' she said, and the sound of the catch in her voice surprised her.

'François?'

'He's well... yes, he's well,' she murmured, her cold lips making an effort to shape the words, 'He happens to be away for two days. What a pity!'

'Yes,' he said, 'and I'm leaving tomorrow.'

'What a pity,' she repeated mechanically.

'Do you still live in South America?'

He had sat down beside her with a brief 'may I?' and was looking at her with sustained attention.

'Did you not get married over there?'

He half-closed his eyes, a habitual weary gesture of his; he seemed to be looking into the depths of his heart. He had large golden-brown, almost yellow eyes. Amid his plumpened face there was still a strange beauty to his eyes, which contrasted with his long hollow temples, his thinly sculpted nose and swollen jowls.

'No,' he repeated slowly. Raising his gaze, he fixed his eyes on the mirror tilted above the bar. 'It feels strange coming back here after so many years. And nothing's changed... That little May is the image of Doris when she was young. But I was told the black man doesn't come any more. That's a pity…'

'Have you not been back to Paris in twenty years?'

'I have, occasionally… Two weeks, ten days, passing through…'

'And you never came to see us?'

He didn't apologise; he remained silent; he slowly turned Thérèse's empty glass between his hands.

'Are you waiting for someone?' he asked.

'Not at all. I was thinking of having lunch here.'

'Here?'

He pulled a face. A few men came in and sat down on the high stools at the bar.

'Would you like to come and have lunch with me?' Raymond asked abruptly.

'Of course,' she said slowly, 'That's very nice of you… I'd love that…'

'Where?'

'Well,' she smiled, 'wherever you like, my dear.'

'Let's go then.'

One by one he gathered up the packages left on the bench. When she had got up, he looked at her intently, a profound expression in his gaze. Then, without saying a word, he too got up and followed her. She walked briskly. Outside the midday heat fell upon their shoulders as soon as they had crossed the threshold.

'Unbearable, isn't it?' he said.

His car was parked by the kerb.

'Would you like to go to Ville-d'Avray? There's always a bit of cool air coming from the lake.'

'Let's go there.'

He sat behind the wheel. They set off. She turned her eyes away from his broad nape, which she could see between his collar and his hat. He had... that's it... got broader... The years seemed to bind men and women to the ground, fill them up with some kind of heavy substance, bloat them, stuff them with flesh and blood... weigh them down, fasten them with a thousand bonds to the ground to which they would all return... She wound down the window and a sharp wind lashed her face. She gazed out absent-mindedly at the impoverished rural hinterland of Paris, its fields gnawed at and yellowed by the sun, its houses once pink, now blackened by smoke. They drove through Saint-Cloud, and only at the fork in the road, when they had passed the viaduct and when she saw the deep green valley that goes from Saint-Cloud to Ville-d'Avray stretch out before her, did she feel her strange numbness dissipate.

'Once,' said Cazeneuve, without turning his head, 'we came here at night with you and your husband.'

Thérèse knitted her brow slightly with a stifled sigh. Yes... One night, with François, a woman who had since died and who was called, what was it?... Solange Saint-Clair... and Raymond... Solange Saint-Clair... The thought of her lovely frail body lying for so many years in the ground, transformed into grass, into long, sinuous roots, dissolved, vanished, made the many intervening years seem even longer.

She remembered that sigh, that 'ah' of satisfaction that they had all breathed as they had passed beneath that dark vault of trees, the same vault into which the car was now driving, a sigh such as the one breathed after the first mouthful of cool water when one is parched by the summer heat. But today the dust was flying in the air, cars were passing them continuously, everything was different. Then the memory suddenly grew so ardent and so vivid that she recoiled as if she really had passed her hand over a naked flame. It had been late... They had gone to drink a bottle of champagne in Ville-d'Avray. It was almost dawn. The top of the car had been folded back. They were driving very slowly, drinking in the fresh morning air with relish. Her white dress... She had to concentrate a little to remember it, but suddenly the image of herself, the woman she was back then appeared. She was beautiful back then... or at least young, radiant, triumphant, feeling the loving admiration of men soaring in her wake. François had held her tight against him, had pressed her against him all along the road, caressing her with his beautiful, warm, nervous hand. And the other man?... She remembered the passionate excitement of that silent plea directed at him: 'Look at me. Look at me. Love me.' That urge to be loved awakened desire, affection. And now? Maybe now, still?...

'I'm forty,' she thought.

That night, twenty years ago, Raymond had looked at her, and there had been nothing more. Now he didn't speak or laugh. He remained silent and a little sombre. She remembered his face turned towards her, that strange, troubled questioning look in his eyes. 'Maybe both of us were simply a little drunk?... He probably wasn't thinking about me. He wasn't thinking about anything… Maybe… But maybe he did love me, want me? Who knows?'

In Ville-d'Avray they had found themselves alone for a moment. Paper lanterns had been glowing in the trees. François and Solange had gone ahead to the water's edge. She remembered Solange's laughter.

'Ah, we're sinking over here.'

It had got cooler, almost cold. She had felt weary. She had stretched out her bare arm over the table; Raymond had gently taken and lifted her hand. He had lifted it up gently and let it fall with a short sigh. Then for quite some time he had brushed his fingers over her rings.

And from this insignificant touch, which wasn't even an ordinary caress, such a murky heat had risen that even now, after all those years, she could still feel its fierce burn. And what about him? What was he thinking about now?

He raised his hand in a gesture towards the white houses: 'Ville-d'Avray…'

Like long ago, they pulled up beside a narrow painted wooden door. A path led to a terrace sheltered by a thatched roof, a kind of long gallery of separate booths forming a series of little alcoves, all opening out onto the lake.

'This way, Madame,' the headwaiter said.

She went in. The partitions were covered with plaited straw and decorated with large mirrors, all of which were diamond-etched with names. It was a quaint old house dating from the time when people travelled from Paris to

Ville-d'Avray in a victoria or a calèche, and some women who were probably very old or dead, all gone, those Coralies, Marguerites, Alphonsines still kept a little of their strange charm. The dates... She moved closer and read them: *1886, 1889.* She sighed and brushed her hand over the glittering surface.

'Would you like to see the menu?' Raymond Cazeneuve said.

The headwaiter, leaning forward slightly, was looking at Raymond and Thérèse with a piercing attentiveness, seemingly searching their faces for those distinctive traits that might betray their tastes, their preferences, as well as their ages and social statuses, seemingly adding all these together in order to deduce signs as to what dishes he should offer them.

'Crayfish, Monsieur? I'd recommend a stack of crayfish to start.'

'In this season? Do you think so?' Raymond said.

His gaze moved back and forth between the menu and the headwaiter.

'What do you think, my dear?'

She turned away slowly; she was taking off her hat in front of the mirror, and the names and the dates engraved on the surface, lit up by the sun, glittered between her and the image of a tired, ageing woman.

Instinctively she lowered her eyelids and turned her head slightly, giving her face the angle that long ago best suited her.

'Why not?' she said automatically, playing with the felt ribbon knotted on the brim of her hat.

'They are superb,' the headwaiter said. 'Brioches à la bohémienne to follow, Monsieur?'

'What's that?'

'Hollowed out brioches,' said the headwaiter, lightly sketching in the air with his two hands delicately cupped in the shape of a bowl or an amphora, 'filled with foie gras mousse, finely chopped truffles, mushrooms—a speciality of the house.'

'That sounds good,' said Thérèse, whom he was questioning with his eyes.

She felt vaguely numb. She had sat down, leaning her head on the back of the straw armchair. A crisp wind was blowing in her face. The mirrors reflected the swaying willow branches and the deep, rapid eddies in the water.

'And to follow? Poulard with fine asparagus tips or coq au Chambertin?'

'Coq au Chambertin, right, Thérèse? And afterwards, of course, the house strawberries, their masterpiece, strawberries with fine champagne and cream.'

'A stack of crayfish, brioches à la bohémienne, coq au Chambertin and strawberries,' the headwaiter repeated softly.

'And could you send the sommelier over?'

They were left alone. Their eyes met in a flash. A strange little smile parted Raymond's lips. He wanted to speak but hesitated and turned his head away.

'It's been so long,' he said eventually. 'Have you come back here since?'

'No, never.'

'Charming place,' he said in a lighter tone, 'dated, but charming.'

The sommelier came up to the table and presented the wine menu. Raymond studied it carefully. Whenever he was silent, a strange fine line contracted the middle of his brow.

'They have a one-of-a-kind champagne, a 1904 Giesler. How about a champagne lunch? This one,' he said, underlining with a fingernail the name on the menu.

Once again they were alone.

'I'll regret having missed François for the rest of my life,' he said.

'But you'll be back, won't you? He'll very much regret it too, I'm sure.'

'I won't be back for another three years now.'

They fell silent, searching vaguely for a topic of conversation and finding none. 'Twenty years…' they thought in unison with a bizarre shiver, as if they could only now measure the years that had passed.

'You haven't changed at all, Thérèse,' he said slowly.

'Ah, my dear…' she murmured, laughing a little.

She didn't finish the sentence. Without thinking, she tilted her head back towards the shade, where the sun didn't run the risk of shining down through her hair, which was still a dark golden-brown, to illuminate the multitude of silver threads around her temples.

The stack of scarlet crayfish appeared on a silver plate, and the fine old Giesler was poured.

'My God,' she said as she took the first mouthful, laughing, 'I didn't realise I was so hungry…'

'They're small, but superb,' Raymond said with satisfaction.

They cracked under his teeth, and for the very first time Thérèse noticed his short white teeth, which seemed to enjoy biting and crunching. His lips... They hadn't changed... a little dry and as if always thirsty, thinly but beautifully shaped. She was suddenly seized by a painful, voluptuous shiver.

'How silly, God, how silly,' she thought with frustration. The sudden brief rush of desire subsided. He had caught her gaze lifted towards him, and for a moment she thought she saw a little tremor of desire, quickly repressed, pass over his lips... A moment... Or was it the chilled champagne rising in burning waves to her heart and temples? 'I just want to know if he loved me. I want to know... After twenty years it doesn't matter anymore, true... What good would finding out do? And yet, how many nights I've spent thinking of him, dreaming of him...' She thought of those unfaithful dreams with a latent swell of remorse. 'He's aged, changed... Did he love me? It would be so easy to ask him... That's all distant now, finished, forgotten.'

'More champagne? It's good, isn't it?'

'Yes,' she mumbled, moving her glass forward.

She drank quickly.

'Speak, will you, speak,' she suddenly thought fiercely. 'I love you!...'

She held the glass between her two trembling hands and continued to drink, her eyes half-closed. Her face had blushed furiously, and she saw Raymond's sad, attentive eyes up close. What was he thinking about? Some dark revenge? Some exquisite little pleasure of revenge against the woman he had once desired (one evening, perhaps, one single evening?…), who was too young, too happy, too overjoyed to notice?

'These crayfish burn your lips,' he remarked.

He passed the tips of his delicate fingers over his lips, and she thought she could feel the burning taste of pepper and alcohol on her own mouth.

'It's a pleasant place, but the climate there is dreadful…'

She realised he was talking about America and that she had probably responded.

'Sometimes at dusk, during the winter, there are these gusts of icy wind that sweep through the streets. But I love the spring and summer. You sleep a great deal in summer. It's very satisfying. There are only two sources of satisfaction in life: food and sleep.'

She laughed joylessly.

'Really?'

'What about you?'

'Me?'

'Yes. What do you do? Here I am telling you all about my life…'

'Your travels, for the most part.' (She delicately lifted the golden top of her brioche.) 'What about me… Well, I eat, I sleep, and I also go to my dressmaker's to try on dresses; in January I buy tablecloths and tea towels at the linen fairs, I get out of Paris for three weeks every year in summer; I read, I go to the picture house… And there you are. That's all.'

He raised his eyebrows with a smile.

'Happiness is like a holiday by the seaside during a rainy summer, with the sunshine only coming on the last day, and that's enough to make you want to go through it all over again.'

'Happiness,' she repeated softly.

She fell silent. Through the large open bay window she looked out at the beautiful lake in which willows grew.

'On a long Sunday…' she said eventually with a smile.

He wanted to say something, but a mocking, melancholic expression suddenly spread over his features. He shrugged his shoulders almost imperceptibly.

'One more,' he said, taking between his spoon and fork a soft golden brioche, a fragrant mousse escaping through its slightly cracked crust. 'These are delicious…'

'You enjoy eating, I see?'

'Very much so. The food is vile over there, but I've kept an old lady from Béarn in my service, an excellent cook. I love eating and, above all, drinking,' he added with a little laughter as he held up the bottle which appeared heavier in the mirror. 'More?'

She drank avidly; her temples were throbbing; a strange, primitive well-being came over her. 'Love?' she thought. She moved her shoulders wearily. 'It's about time…' The headwaiter came up to the table, followed by another waiter carrying the coq au Chambertin with truffles and fine slivers of golden-brown mushrooms; the sauce had the colour of rust, gold, fire. Raymond breathed in the aroma with a smile.

'Divine…'

But the food and the wine made him appear paler. She looked at him more closely and reflected that his blanched, slightly puffy cheeks, his heavy eyelids and the dark bluish-purple rings under his eyes lent his face the mask of someone suffering from a heart condition. But in that pale, heavy face with its eyes half-closed, his thin, thirsty lips remained unchanged, cruel and loving.

It was almost three o'clock. The sun was shedding light on the water in a different way from before. From one shoreline to another a glittering block of golden light seemed to cross the lake from side to side.

'What a beautiful day…' Thérèse murmured.

She pushed her plate away. She turned away slightly and put her hand on the warm wooden balustrade. In the neighbouring little booth, from where until now the monotonous humming of two voices could be heard, a curious silence had descended, but this was suddenly broken by a woman's sigh and a little shriek, like one of those involuntary groans that escapes from the depths of a dream.

She gazed absentmindedly at the flashes of light sparkling on the side of her glass. He was not drinking; he was also holding his glass between both hands. Eventually he raised it slowly to his lips and drank with a little sigh.

'This is better than love…'

She looked up, surprised by his strange, harsh, deep voice. For a moment they looked each other in the eyes, spitefully, measuring their powers. A sort of fire, regret, anger spread over their features, but he turned his face away.

'Salad?' he asked politely.

She shook her head without answering.

'Has François changed much?' he asked with the same courteous indifference.

'Yes,' she said briefly, 'he's changed too…'

He laughed a little, and once again a strange, spiteful expression spread over his lips, as if he were thinking, 'That's how it goes, my dear… it's all over…'

'Stupid fool of a woman,' she suddenly thought, 'he never loved me!'

Once again she looked at him surreptitiously. She felt something like hatred towards him, a kind of irritation, the urge to answer him in an unpleasant, cutting way, and at the same time a feeling of bittersweet love swelled up in her heart.

The door opened after a light, discreet knock. The headwaiter came in, pushing in front of him on a serving trolley an enormous crystal bowl filled to the brim with strawberries and thick cream, through which the ardent golden rivulets of a fragrant old champagne brandy flowed.

'A lunch fit for a king,' Thérèse said.

He gently shrugged his shoulders.

'I'm glad I was able to convince you to come,' he

said in a measured undertone. 'I'm glad to have seen you again…'

'Well, so am I, my dear.'

She tried to smile, stretched her hand out to him like long ago, took her glass of champagne and brought it slowly to her lips. She saw his gaze come down on her delicately, perfectly shaped hand. 'Does he remember?' And she was surprised by the savage beating of her heart, which filled her with anger. 'What nonsense!… And what on earth should he remember? Nothing!… Not even a caress… He touched my rings, not my skin…'

But immediately she saw once more his face tilted to the side, the two lit lamps on the table, their pink paper cones and the heat, the scent, the light wind of that May night…

She turned away as tears were welling up in her eyes. She stared at the lake. Four o'clock and already the September day no longer had the radiance of true summer. Already the birds were passing through a paler sky with confused cries; they flew quickly, criss-crossed one another like figures in a ballet, then some of them rose even higher while others fell like stones towards the lake. A silver fish glittered, or was it an eddy, a reflection in the water? Some small greyish clouds were stretched over the horizon, veiling the sun. 'My youth,' thought Thérèse with desperation, 'my short, my stupid, my only youth! And what's the use of knowing now whether he loved me? What's the use? Even if he were to tell me now, "Yes, you guessed it, I did love you…"' In spite of herself, her heart beating fast, she tilted her head as if to listen to these words whispered in her ear: love, loving… words she would never hear again… 'In spite of it all, that would only be the past. What I'd still like to call my own isn't that, but the spring, that May night, François's loving face and the warm, trembling hands of… the other man.' And now he was sitting in front of her, heavy, tired, sardonic; he was eating his strawberries. 'He's absolutely right. Drinking, eating, sleeping, that's all there is.'

She took her spoon and swallowed a strawberry with some effort. They had been steeped at length in alcohol and cream; they were enormous, fragrant, deliciously soft.

'Oh my, they are superb, I must say…'

'Aren't they?'

She drank a little more, and gradually the knot tightening her throat loosened imperceptibly; once again she felt overwhelmed by a dark, primitive sense of well-being tainted by a sad resignation.

'Yes, my dear,' he repeated, 'nothing can beat a fine dish, a good bottle, a glass of some fine aged wine or spirit warmed in the hollow of your hand, the fragrance of a cigar—'

'You can smoke, you know,' she interrupted.

'And for you?'

She took a cigarette from the half-open case, threw back her head and gazed for some time at the blue smoke, which was floating and unfolding in the air and rising towards the mirror, and through which appeared

Lunch in September

Cora, 1885…, Lola, 1890, Ville-d'Avray, in the month of May.

The headwaiter brought in the coffee and carefully lit the small stove, whose transparent little flame merged with the daylight but had a beautifully vivid deep blue colour cut with flashes of gold. He lit Raymond's cigar, placed two balloon glasses before him and gently poured out some old smooth golden armagnac, the fragrance of which filled the little booth.

'You should throw something across your shoulders,' Raymond advised. 'You're dressed very lightly, and it's getting cold all of a sudden.'

It was indeed cold. The clouds had veiled the sun; a sunbeam shone down over the tops of the red trees; a little bush on the lake appeared completely red, a dark red like wine or blood. Some men were walking along the shoreline, their fishing rods over their shoulders.

'Jea-a-anne!…' someone called out, a woman's voice.

Silence, then the same distant voice: 'Jea-a-anne… Put on your coat!… The wind is getting cooler!…'

Raymond had got up. He threw his coat over Thérèse's shoulders with a laugh.

'Believe me, it feels like autumn. It's crazy, it's barely five o'clock.'

'Already!' she said. 'Oh, it's awfully late…'

'Would you like to go home?'

She hesitated a little, looked at the waning sky and reflected that the housemaid must be waiting for her to finish tidying the cupboards.

'Yes, please, Raymond, I'd like to go home.'

He turned away, pressed his finger on the bell and said in an undertone to the headwaiter coming in, 'The bill.'

Thérèse picked up her bag mechanically and pulled out the flat little golden box that held her blusher and powder cases, her other bits of makeup and her mirror. She took the little mirror, sighed, blew lightly on the tarnished surface and looked at herself. She saw a face that had grown pale. Underneath the powder, which had now faded away, the blusher on her cheekbones had turned into a garish stain. She saw the worried line of her mouth, her puffy cheeks, her weary eyes, her wrinkles… To other eyes she was still young. To other eyes her face might still be attractive, might still seem delicate and pure… She alone—and probably he—could see the damage.

Raymond returned to her.

'Are you not going to catch a cold? It's extraordinary how the weather's changed… We'll have to wind up the windows…'

He held her hat out to her and she put it back on slowly, focusing on controlling the slight nervous tremor in her hands. The mirror was full of shadows now; the sun had moved; the names, the dates, were disappearing.

'You'll come back here,' said Raymond, 'with François…'

'Of course,' she said.

They walked out. The car drove away.

The day was still bright, despite everything; in the veiled sunlight, in the shade of the trees spread over the fields, in the pale bluish reflection of the road, dusk and autumn could be sensed.

In Saint-Cloud their car had to come to a halt and joined the queue behind others. Children were handing out flowers. From a basket held toward Raymond took out a bouquet of short-stemmed roses with fresh, moist petals.

'Thérèse…'

He said nothing else.

They set off again. Before long they had passed through the suburbs and had reached Paris. He asked for her address. She soon recognised the street next to her own, the red shopfront of the chemist, the picture house, the quiet little avenue where she lived.

'Thank you.'

He took her hand and kissed it. It was a strange kiss, longer perhaps than it ought to have been, and his lips, pressed against her fingers, were trembling slightly. She slowly drew her hand away, looked at him and saw up close that face, now heavier, sardonic and indifferent, and his thin, thirsty lips.

'Farewell,' she murmured.

He started and furrowed his brow with a disgruntled, distressed pout.

'Until we meet again, you mean,' he eventually said softly. 'Maybe we'll see each other again one day…'

He opened the door for her. She got out of the car. The door closed behind her back with a dull thud. She heard the revving of the car starting up again, and the sound drifted away and petered out as it advanced along the empty street.

IN CONFIDENCE

It's better this way,' she thought. 'Firstly, one must submit to God's will. Secondly, what could I expect from life? I'm not young any more. I have no family. (The Lamberts don't count,' she added, and as soon as she remembered them a sour, tense expression came over her face: she was the Lamberts' poor relative and never forgot it.) 'I'm a laughing stock to them! An old schoolmistress, I certainly don't do them proud. I'm poor. I have no friends. If I should die from the operation, death will spare me years of pitiful old age,' she continued, attempting through resigned, rational, Christian thoughts to impose calm on her dismal heart, which was faltering with fear and apprehension.

She had wanted to walk back from the doctor's practice to the rue Monge, where she lived. In so doing she proved herself to have courage: when all else fails, final salvation lies in that faint flicker of pride.

Blanche Lajunie braved distress and fatigue, walked briskly, held her head high and glanced with great pride and defiance at the passers-by, as if she were thinking, 'See now, I'm just a poor, lonely old maid! But I don't need anyone! I refuse all help. A good many women in my situation would fall ill or rush back home to lock themselves away and cry. Thank God I don't feel the need to cry! Life's not worth all that regret. Yes, you can push me around because you're nimbler and stronger than me! You can make fun of my outdated hat and my old wrinkled face, but I have more dignity and more courage than you!'

The indifferent crowd pushed her on. It was noon. All the shops and offices were closing their doors. Everyone was rushing. No one even glanced at her. No one would recognise this supreme effort of the propriety and dignity she was imposing on herself... But she would not give up. She would walk home. At the hour of her death she would be able to think in all honesty, 'I was my own mistress until the very last day. That day when I learnt I was at risk from a serious, perhaps life-threatening operation—doubtless life-threatening (I can sense it)—was no different for me to any other day. I didn't even let myself take a taxi. I was brave. I asked no one for help. I've always had a particular admiration for all those ordinary women who traipse on until the very end and toil and moil without complaining and only stop to die, those women of whom one can say, "They're tough…" As for me…'

It was only at the doctor's that she had had a moment of weakness: she had shed a few tears. He had the soft voice and indifferent expression of someone whose job it is to feign interest in another's fate. 'My undivided attention and all my expertise are yours,' the voice and expression seemed to say, 'and yours alone—for ten or fifteen minutes. Don't ask any more of me. I'm up to my eyeballs. Others are waiting for me behind that door, you see. Above all don't ask me for even a crumb of compassion or an atom of love. Where would we find ourselves, Mademoiselle, if we had to show compassion for everyone who asks us for it? A small-time neighbourhood doctor with youth still on his side might… But me! At over a hundred francs per visit, don't ask for my compassion. That would be an insult.'

'It's an operation we perform daily,' he had said, 'so trust us. Don't you have any family? Let's hear that heart. Have you been feeling tired lately? Not at all, not at all, your heart is fine. Don't worry about it.'

Perhaps by virtue of her career as a schoolmistress, she had acquired a certain skill in penetrating the thoughts of others. It seemed to her that she could read the doctor's mind while he was examining her, while he carefully placed his head against his patient's meagre chest: 'No family, that's a pity. It's so easy to find an understanding ear in a relative, one who won't get too upset. An heir, for example…' But she had already understood.

Yes, she had understood. It was up to her to bear this, as she had borne sorrow and loneliness; it was up to her to come to terms with this glimpse of truth; it was up to her to wait; it was up to her to watch the streets of Paris, the bright azure sky, the sun, those suitcase-laden cars leaving for the countryside, for the Easter holidays, and to think, 'This or that month, this or that day I may no longer be alive. Me? Oh! Is this really happening to me?' For fear of death does not spare the humble: there is no prey too weak for that terror, for that rapacious hunter.

Nevertheless, she had regained her composure at the doctor's after that first moment, the first shiver of animal terror; she had calmly discussed the cost of the operation and had noted with an unfaltering hand the addresses of the 'middle-class' hospitals and sanatoriums as well as the agreed date for the operation, as if she could have forgotten.

The rue Monge was still far away. Blanche Lajunie now only walked on with difficulty. She sat down on a bench. Now alone, she finally let a weary, bitter expression spread over her face. However, during her classes and lessons, when she was commanding the students' attention, when with sarcasm, threats, a false serenity or clever dialectics she penetrated their intentions, their thoughts, their lies, she still seemed sprightly, energetic and quite formidable. She was fifty years old, there was a great stiffness to her posture and she had that abrupt and almost masculine manner that habitual self-sufficiency and poverty can lend to women. Her eyes were bright;

she must have been pretty once, but excessive weight loss had wrecked the proportions of her face: only the haughty bridge of her nose held firm amid the overall sagging of her features; her eyelids were heavy and withered; her pince-nez, which, out of what was left of her pride in her appearance, she used only for reading, had ploughed two small reddish furrows in the flesh at the corners of her eyes. She was dressed quite correctly but in that imperceptibly ridiculous fashion that makes a woman stand out not only because she is poor but also because she never goes out and no longer knows what people are wearing. Thus her black felt hat, the brim turned up at the side with a blue Galalith buckle, followed the trend, but self-consciously and a season behind, while her dark coat (a well-worn item) was downright obsolete and odd. She knew this; it upset her, and those embarrassed glances she sometimes cast over her dresses, her old gloves, her clumpy shoes, revealed better than the still-beautiful contours of her mouth and hands that indeed she had once been pretty.

She had lowered her eyes and folded her hands over her knees. It was a spring day and already so fine and so hot that it seemed like high summer. That burst of light, that gentle warmth in the air both delighted and wounded her; the faces and voices of the passers-by irritated her. She found herself in the university quarter. Youth was more pervasive here than anywhere else; it reigned; it filled the benches, the streets and the squares. Mademoiselle Lajunie disliked youth; it was her job to curb it, to scold it, to treat it as an enemy. Those gangs of boys and girls with berets on their heads and satchels under their arms, who blocked the pavements, who laughed, whose airy, insolent voices rang in her ears, annoyed her. In order to escape from them, she mustered the strength to get up, hail the passing AX bus and heave her trembling legs onto the platform. Have a little patience now, a little courage. Just a few more minutes. Here's the stop for the rue Monge. A few more steps. Then she would be home.

The small apartment in which she lived was cheap and funereal but very clean. It was on the second floor and overlooked the courtyard. She had fully set the kitchen table that very morning for her midday meal: she took her lunch at home three times a week; on the other days she ate in one of her students' homes. She lit the gas, but when she noticed the cutlet, which was still raw and bleeding and needed to be put over the heat, a moment of faintness suddenly came over her. She hastily shut the cutlet away in a cupboard, boiled up some water and, with a cup of tea in her hand and some crispbreads on a plate, entered the dining room. She slowly took off her hat; her hands were still trembling. She sat down at her usual place, facing the window, and tried to focus her thoughts on the tasks to be done that day.

Little Colette Lambert, her cousin's daughter, was due to visit her from four until five o'clock for a lesson in French literature. The interval between lunch and the time she had to receive Colette was usually filled with a private mathematics class in Neuilly. But that day, fearing she might be delayed at the doctor's, she had kept only her appointment with Colette and had cancelled her other students' lessons: Colette was very behind in literature and history. 'Those little girls are hopeless when it comes to anything that demands responsiveness or imagination,' Mademoiselle Lajunie thought. Yet she was drawn to these lazy and unruly schoolchildren like a rider to a wild horse, to break it in against its will, to instil her own determination in it and, finally, for their own good, to vanquish it. Once this task had been successfully completed, the student could change master, just as a horse can be sold: Mademoiselle Lajunie would consider herself satisfied.

She was free then until four o'clock. She sighed. It wasn't free time she needed. She envied in that moment the fate of worn-out housewives, of women encumbered by families, of those women who literally never had 'time to think', as the saying goes. Running from one part of the city to another, waiting for the bus, climbing the stairs of the old Left Bank buildings that have no lifts, correcting homework, dictating summaries of historical events, all of which still ceded too much ground to one's inner life, whereas a woman stupefied by the shouting and crying of children, distracted by household chores, by meals, has succeeded in suppressing within herself, Mademoiselle Lajunie mused, every desire and every regret, and that's certainly half the battle won!

She had nonetheless often said and thought that she was glad not to be married, not to have children. She had lived a dignified and independent life. She was well travelled. She had lived in Italy for five years; she had been the governess of the Spanish ambassador's two daughters. She had taken her students to Spain. She had spent some time in Switzerland and England. She had begun her career at a very young age, in Russia, before the war... She had therefore had the opportunity to break into social circles different from her own, and which a person of her class and financial circumstances only rarely had the chance to experience.

'How dull and miserable life with a husband and children would be!' she thought. 'My parents were almost peasants. Who could I have married?'

She remembered the village in Lorraine in which she was born, and which she had left when she was sixteen. 'No, I regret nothing. And yet with a husband and children, at least a memory, a faithful representation of you is kept after your death. As for me! I have no relatives left, not a single friend from my youth. No one remembers me the way I used to be.'

She imagined the reactions of her neighbours, the students' parents, the Lamberts themselves, who had already considered her old ten years ago, upon her return from Italy. What would they say? 'Poor girl, poor old dear...'

'A broken record blaring out notions about English and grammar during mathematics classes, that's what I am in their eyes. That's what I'll always be. I'll be down in the ground, I'll be as if I had never been, and this caricature of me, the image of a bitter old maid, will live on in all those memories. And yet I was a woman... Ah, none of that should matter to me! Better still! I ought to find in it some kind of ironic pleasure. Until now I've been glad to lose sight of everyone who knew me when I was young. I didn't find it disagreeable to look at pretty Madame Lange or little Francine's mother and think, "Do you pity me? You think I've always been old, ugly and lonely. But I was more beautiful than you, more loved than you!" And the young girls! Ah, all those happy, cheeky little misses! Roselyne, Nicole, Annette, I know and I feel that they sometimes wonder if, once upon a time, I could have ever been young like them. They're at the age of their first rendezvous and puppy love romances. I don't envy them. I know all too well how all that ends. I know the taste of the tears they'll cry. Poor little silly geese!... But I'm a weak woman. I'd like to tug them by the arm and tell them, 'Wait! Look! Listen to me! Don't push me away! I was like you.'

'*Et in Arcadia ego*,' she murmured mechanically, and the Latin quotation, through a force of habit acquired from her teaching, mysteriously soothed her. Giving her pain a concise and exquisite classical form was, in spite of it all, some consolation. She felt better.

She finished tidying away a few things and corrected a student's homework. At four o'clock she heard her young cousin ring the doorbell.

The Lamberts were rich, staid people. By a tacit agreement, reference was never made between them and Mademoiselle Lajunie to the extent of their relatedness, which was nonetheless quite close: Lambert was Mademoiselle Lajunie's great-nephew. He had made a fortune after the war.

Lambert and his wife appreciated Blanche Lajunie's qualities as a teacher and educator: she alone had succeeded in getting their eldest son through his final-year exams, after he had failed them twice previously. She now acted as fifteen-year-old Colette's private tutor. The Lamberts, when they spoke of the old maid, said in chorus that she was learned, intelligent, 'but dry, cold and selfish', concluded Madame Lambert with rancour, recalling certain of her cousin's acerbic remarks. Blanche Lajunie was very eager to let it be known that she stuck to her plain speaking even with her rich parents and was not averse to irritating anyone. Indeed, irritating others was an innate gift of hers, one with which not everyone is blessed. She was a quick-witted soul; a certain malevolence brought out the qualities of that soul even more, just as the juice of a lemon gives full expression to the flavour of a dish. It was strange: while making her way to such and such a student's home she sometimes happened to be moved by a reflection, a memory, a piece of writing, or to feel in her heart that bittersweet emotion that awakens in city-dwellers' souls during the first days of spring. Then she was all tenderness, all love, ready to bond with a dog or a child, thinking vaguely of adopting a stray cat, of planting flowers on her windowsill; her step was heavier; she was weary. She arrived in an unfamiliar house, where everyone visibly had worries and pleasures that she would never experience, and which they jealously kept to themselves; the little girls' laughter stopped suddenly upon her ringing the doorbell; she could guess so well what they were saying to each other: 'Here's that old Lajunie, coming to bother us with her participles and her Racine tragedies!' Straight away she felt the desire to challenge them, to combat them, to impose her will on them, to make them pay for their joy, which was unknown to her, with little put-downs, with ironic remarks, and to say nasty things (nonetheless always true) to their parents about their children's behaviour or effort, and this got to work on her like a tonic. She even felt better physically. Outside, she pushed away with the end of her closed umbrella the little ones that came running into her, throwing themselves against her skirt.

Likewise, that day, as soon as Colette entered, Mademoiselle Lajunie's sadness, without disappearing, seemed lightened, and all that remained apparent was a mocking contempt and that singular need to master others, to make them obey, to mould their souls, which, tempered by her sense of fairness and a certain dignity of character, made her an excellent teacher.

Colette Lambert, in a light-coloured dress, her arms bare, threw her books on the table and greeted Mademoiselle Lajunie. She was a little girl of fifteen years, still a child in her face, already a woman in view of her waist and hips and certain movements of her body. Her cheeks were flushed by her hurried pace and the afternoon heat. Her eyes were ingenuous and bold, her hair chestnut, but in the family they still called it blonde out of habit. Children change so quickly, and their parents realise so slowly! The transformations of adolescence are long complete before the parents notice anything; they notice neither the young girl's curls that have lost their golden colour, that are not even curls any more, but light, tousled hair, nor the eyes that no longer reveal innocent playfulness, but curiosity and a confused turmoil. Mademoiselle Lajunie herself, who had known Colette when she was still very young, spoke, when she addressed her, to a vanished image, to the reflection of a child who no longer existed.

Colette passed over her brow her little handkerchief, which was rolled up into a ball.'It's hot, you know,' she said. 'It's so nice in the Jardin du Luxembourg!'

'Is that where you're coming from?' asked Mademoiselle Lajunie, gazing at her coldly.

She had asked her to revise Madame de Sévigné's letter about the autumn leaves and the summary of the Quarrel of the Ancients and the Moderns before coming over, but that little girl…

'Is that where you're coming from?' she repeated.

Colette batted her eyelids lightly.

'Yes, Mademoiselle Blanche,' she said with a sly, distant expression.

She slowly took her books and notebooks out of her satchel and hesitated.

'May I please sit where you're sitting?'

'Facing the window? If you wish… You have such an obsession about sitting there! You'll have the sunshine in your eyes.'

'The sun? It doesn't shine much in your eyes,' Colette murmured.

'I hate her so much!' she thought. 'My God, I hate her so much! I wonder if it's a sin to hate someone so much. I wish she'd break her leg. I wish she'd die. She's ugly, she's old, she's horrible. And I particularly can't stand the way she puts on airs! She's proud of her little bit of knowledge, all the little things she's swotted up on, but she doesn't know how to do anything really good or useful or important. She can't do flower arranging or dress well or laugh.'

She looked at her hatefully, but that face itself was a living reminder of final-year exams, essays, marks every three months; she turned her eyes away.

'Let's see that homework.'

'Yes, Mademoiselle Blanche.'

Colette had always been a very weak student, but Mademoiselle Lajunie thought that for some time now she had seemed to be making an effort to work harder. She herself had asked her parents to send her twice a week to Mademoiselle Lajunie as a replacement for the single lesson her relative used to give on Thursday mornings in the Lamberts' house on the rue La Fontaine.

Colette sat down opposite Mademoiselle Lajunie, opened her book at the appropriate page and 'pretended to learn', in the words of her teacher, who could tell the difference between that apparent docility, those occasionally correct answers, and real work.

'Colette, you're not listening to me! Come on now, poppet, I can't be cheating your parents out of their money. It's all well and good to want to learn, as you've shown the desire to do, since you yourself have insisted on taking more classes, but that's not enough. You must put some heart, some thought into it... You haven't heard a word of what I've just said...'

'I have! You were saying, "Vauvenargues takes up gainst La Rochefoucauld the defence of Man, who by then had fallen into disrepute in the eyes of all thinkers."'

'And what does that mean? Come on now, it's not a question of just repeating what I say like a parrot...'

'And what is she daydreaming about?' thought Mademoiselle Lajunie, looking exasperatedly at Colette's eyes, big grey eyes rimmed with dark circles gazing at the sky.

'Colette!... For heaven's sake!... What are you looking at outside that window?'

'Me? Nothing,' Colette said swiftly.

She was looking at the sun on the wall opposite. The light was falling slowly, softly; it was going to reach the open window, that window where a young boy with beautiful dishevelled hair studied at the same time, alone in his bedroom. She didn't know his name but she saw him at each of her lessons (and why else would she have asked for extra classes?).

He was not yet there today. He would come. They would look at each other, smiling. He looked to be sixteen or seventeen years old. He was handsome. He had slender, tanned cheeks and black hair. She thought about him endlessly. Upon leaving Mademoiselle Lajunie's every evening she lingered on the street, near the house... Perhaps she would catch sight of him again? He had never dared meet her but she knew he loved her, she was certain he liked her. Until now she had only loved Clark Gable and Robert Taylor, or certain characters from books, or even faces born of her own dreams, her own desires. For the first time a living boy with beautiful hair... What colour were his eyes? She had not yet seen him today. She would have to make the lesson drag on. She made her best effort to do so: she wrote slowly; she half yawned as she clenched her little jaw; she answered reluctantly, clumsily, lazily, so that she heard Mademoiselle Lajunie say, 'Would you mind repeating that, please?'

The schoolboy's books awaited him in a tidy pile on the table, in front of the window. He would come. Yet it was five o'clock. What to do? The lesson was over. She got up, got her satchel in order, looking desperately for an excuse, a pretext to stay there a little longer.

'Are you going out, Mademoiselle Blanche?' she asked.

'No. Why?'

'No reason. Do you not have any other lessons tonight?'

'No other lessons... no...'

'Do you know, I thought—'

'I'm a little tired today,' Mademoiselle Blanche said with an imperceptible sigh.

'Tired? You do seem tired,' said Colette, who for the first time genuinely saw a human expression on the face that she found so unbearable. 'But what are you going to do all alone?' she asked, moved by a feeling close to pity, 'Are you going to work?'

'I have a few papers to correct… later…'

'You don't want me to stay with you for a little while?'

'With me?' Mademoiselle Blanche asked.

She blushed. Nothing could be stranger, nothing more irritating than this rush of blood rising to withered cheeks.

'Do you not have anything more interesting to do?' she murmured.

'Of course not,' said Colette, dumbfounded, struck in spite of herself by her own bitter, despairing tone. 'I… I was thinking that you're rather alone and that, as long as you don't have much to do, just this once… Besides,' she continued, 'I have to stop by a friend's house nearby, but she'll only be there waiting for me from six o'clock. So I could stay until then, so long as I don't bother you, of course.'

'You're not bothering me,' said Mademoiselle Lajunie.

She was grateful to Colette for her offer. Of course, it didn't count for much, this child's presence, but still… She suddenly considered that little Colette Lambert was her relative, someone of her own blood, and that there weren't many of them left on this earth. There was a bond between them. She could look for some of her own traits in that youthful face. She had never thought about that. She looked at her now and her heart suddenly skipped a beat. Yes, in the curve of her eyelids, perhaps…

'That's a pretty dress you have, Colette,' she said to her, but coldly, as she said everything.

Colette's surprised, mocking smile clearly meant to say, 'Oh dear, she fancies herself an expert!'

She glanced quickly at the mirror above the fireplace and gazed for a moment at her slender bare arms and pink neck.

'Very nice of you to say so, Mademoiselle Blanche,' she murmured.

'She'll soon be sixteen years old,' Mademoiselle Lajunie thought as she too looked at the smooth, tanned skin of Colette's naked arms, that straight little neck and those long dark eyelashes. She felt admiration, sadness and perhaps, in the hidden depths of her heart, the barely perceptible cruelty that awakens in an elderly woman's soul when face to face with someone young who is neither the flesh of her flesh nor the child of her child: 'You're beautiful, you're young, you laugh,' she seemed to think. 'Well, good for you! But I do wonder what will be left of those rosy cheeks and that laughter when you've lived and loved...'

She was thus alternately drawn to and repulsed by Colette, and this, combined with her weariness and the premonition of her own impending death, which she dreaded, filled her with worry and dredged up old memories to the surface more intensely than ever before.

'At sixteen I had just arrived in Russia,' she thought once more.

'You're a big girl...' she said aloud. 'At your age I was alone in the world... I was already making a living for myself.'

'Ah, yes!' Colette said politely, 'you were in Russia, isn't that so?'

Mademoiselle Lajunie heaved a gentle sigh.

'Yes…'

In Russia… My God! What images came to little Colette's mind as she uttered those simple words, thinking 'when she was sixteen Mademoiselle Lajunie worked as a teacher in Russia'? What did she see? An ugly girl, probably, sad and lonely, exiling herself to go to teach French to little strangers in boarding schools, in dark classrooms. Mademoiselle Lajunie unwittingly let out a chuckle, and her eyes lit up a little.

'I spent the best years of my life in Russia,' she said.

'Really? It was a long time ago, wasn't it?'

'Thirty-four years ago.'

'Oh!' Colette said softly, in a tone that betrayed her incredulity: thirty-four years… (memories from more than thirty years ago, was such a thing possible?… They were lost in the mists of time; she began to lose interest.)

'And you think,' Mademoiselle Lajunie thought with contempt and pity, 'you think that's a long time, do you? Granted, it's more than twice the length of your silly, meaningless existence, but it was yesterday, do you hear me? It was yesterday! And now it's over, it's death! Yes, death! There's no mistaking what I feel. So quick, my God, so quick! That was me, that sixteen-year-old child in a grey dress, her hair in plaits rolled up at the ears, dark blonde plaits like your hair… It was me he held by the hand… It was to me he said," Don't be afraid, stop shaking. Why are you shaking like that?… I won't hurt you. I love you."'

She heard Colette ask distractedly, 'You taught lessons in a classroom?'

'No, I was a governess in the princes' family…'

She fell silent. Even now that name, which for so many years she hadn't uttered, would not come to her lips.

'A Russian name, very difficult to pronounce.'

'Were they nice? Were there any young girls?'

'No, two little boys. Their mother had died. They were raised by their grandmother.'

'And… is it a nice country?'

'It's a beautiful country.'

She had mechanically adopted once more her usual authoritative, slightly contemptuous tone of voice.

'I could tell you some very interesting things about those foreign lands, which you probably won't ever get the chance to know.'

'Why not?' thought Colette, 'I'll go travelling too. Why not? But not to make a living! Not like a boring teacher with glasses. I can just imagine Mademoiselle Lajunie visiting Moscow: "Now, children, this is the hill from where Napoleon watched the city burn in… Come on now, which one of you can tell me the exact date? Careful! Don't give me a wrong answer! Or else no dessert for any of you tonight! "She sees nothing but dates, books, numbers, dust! When I go travelling I won't go looking at those old ruins. I'll look at the people. I won't bring a single book, but I'll talk to the ordinary women, to the sellers in the souks,' she thought, smiling to herself, already seeing herself on the streets of a foreign city, a man on her arm. 'I'll marry a diplomat.'

'I've lived in Saint Petersburg and Moscow,' Mademoiselle Lajunie continued regardless, her gaze lowered, 'I've visited the Crimea, and we used to spend the summer in one of the old princess's estates in Oryol Governorate. It was a superb, very sociable life… And the governesses and tutors over there were part of the family in a way. I went to some spectacular parties. The children's father was called Alexis Nicolaïévitch.'

How weak and powerless her words were!… She uttered them, she heard them ring in her ears and she knew that they held no meaning or charm for Colette, but for her… Ah! for her they were crowned with a halo of poetry and emotion, they were charged with sadness and subtle bitterness but imbued equally with happiness, and they evoked happiness; they recalled the only happiness she had known. Saint Petersburg… the princess's mansion… She could see once again the music room where she had first met Alexis Nicolaïévitch. As happens when old age sets in, when death's door is one step away and a dream miraculously brings back one's bygone youth, she felt her heart beating both with joy and pain, a joy and a pain so intense, so intertwined, that it was impossible to distinguish between them or to grant to each its own empire.

He had entered the white drawing room and had looked at her—her, the little French girl, his children's governess. He was young, he was handsome, he had taken her by the hand, he had smiled at her, and from that moment on she had known what was to come.

'Did you not get cold during the winter?'

'It's a splendid climate,' Mademoiselle Lajunie said in a remarkably shrill, tremulous voice. 'The winters are long and severe, but I never suffered from the cold.'

Suffered from the cold... All the memories she had of that land were warm, thrilling, radiant. The snow would fall, the ground would be frozen, but her blood ran fast and ardently, her body was light and supple, and with her, near her, was the constant presence of a loving man... 'Aliocha,' she thought, calling him for the first time in years by the affectionate nickname that she had first whispered in the secrecy of her heart, in the secrecy of her nights, then one day to him, in his ear, in his arms. Was he still alive? How many times she had asked herself that question!... Had he been killed in the war? Murdered by the Reds after 1917? Was he in exile? Poor, perhaps, poorer than her, old, an invalid m... Whatever fate God had dealt the man she had loved, at least in someone's memory, in someone's heart, Blanche Lajunie's, the image remained of a brilliant officer who had entered a white drawing room one spring day just like this one, thirty-four years ago, who had taken her hand, who had smiled at her...

She blushed; she fixed her hair mechanically in the same swift, gracious way she used to back then. Colette didn't notice anything; she didn't look at her old cousin but made her talk on indulgently, lingering by her side, her eyes focused on the house opposite.

'Tell me more about Russia, Mademoiselle. You talk about it so nicely.'

'I can't explain it,' Mademoiselle Lajunie said, nervously wringing her hands together. 'I can't express it,' she said in a very low voice.

This richness with which her heart was overflowing, these recollections, this love, this lapse of memory, everything that made her a woman different from others, a woman among a thousand other women, everything that makes a human being not only a physical manifestation and a name in a civil register, but a soul—all of this was invisible, inexpressible… and yet…

She was still struggling to maintain her coldness, her neutral tone, intentionally devoid of all emotion.

'Imagine a very flat land, where, unlike in France, your gaze is not interrupted immediately by a hill or the roofs of a village. For hours, by carriage, all you can see are fields and plains. Everywhere is bare and, in winter, everything is covered in snow.'

She saw one image from among a thousand others resurface as she spoke, that of the horses pausing and breathing into the misty air, muffled by the snow. The sky is low and dark, but a pale, cold, celestial light rises from the white ground, illuminating everything with an indeterminate twilight brightness. Then it all dies out; the wind is icy; an unmoving red fire sparkles alone amid a snowdrift. She's on a sleigh with Aliocha. He's holding her by the waist. She lifts the little muff to her lips. She thinks she can still smell the faint scent of fur and rose oil after so many years. She leans her forehead on Aliocha's shoulder.

'Are you happy?' he says softly.

'I was a very good dancer back then…' Mademoiselle Lajunie continued. 'I loved to dance…'

'You? Never!…'

But Colette's naive insolence no longer had the power to irritate the old woman. Yes, she had been happy. Anything in the world could have come to pass, and the worst did come to pass: their parting, thankless toil and, to crown it all, this death awaiting her in a hospital ward or, later, here, in these rooms, alone—but nothing could change the past.

'Of course. I was a good dancer. Are you surprised? But I was sixteen, I was happy. You find that unbelievable, don't you? The possibility of being happy in a foreign land, among strangers, while poor and in a dependent state? But there comes a time…'

She fell silent.

'Ah! I can't carry this with me,' she thought, 'what I was, my truth. Let this girl at least keep its memory, its testimony… I've never talked to anyone about Aliocha. But now I'm going to die. Why not tell her about the past? There's nothing in any of it to be ashamed of. The purest tenderness, the chastest love… And she's at that age when words and love stories have such a resonance that she'll never forget them.'

That was what she wanted above all else: to prolong

for one moment more—for one instant, the span of a generation—that ephemeral memory.

'If I have such a vivid memory of Russia,' she said in a changed tone of voice, 'it's, as you might guess, because I met somebody over there whom I loved and whom I haven't forgotten. I've never told anyone this, Colette,' she said in yet a lower voice, 'but I feel so sad today, so down... I won't be around much longer, sweetheart.'

Colette suppressed with some difficulty a twitch of joy.

Mademoiselle Lajunie wanted to say 'I'm going to have to undergo a serious operation', but she wanted to leave Colette not with a memory that might have aroused pity in her, but one of tenderness and friendship.

'I'm old, and it would be very sweet to know that someone somewhere still remembers me and this old fairytale romance of mine. He was noble and wealthy. I knew that marriage between us would have been, if not impossible, at least all but a folly, almost a miracle, but I still had some hope. One day you'll know this feeling of running into an abyss, into tragedy, into death, your eyes wide open, to know it full well, and yet...'

She fell silent. The memories, too numerous, too sweet, throbbed in her heart and choked her. Meanwhile, Colette, who had been listening to her without hearing her, had stood up and approached the window. As Colette moved, Mademoiselle Lajunie came back to herself and to the present; with a suspicious glance she scanned the facade of the house at which Colette was gazing and saw at the second-floor window a handsome boy of sixteen or seventeen with tanned cheeks and black hair. He was looking at Colette with a smile.

'So that's it!' Mademoiselle Lajunie thought, recalling in a flash Colette's insistence upon staying with her. 'Wretched little brat! So that's it!...'

She slammed the books and notebooks shut.

'Your obedience has been exemplary,' she said sarcastically, 'Thank you for being so devoted as to listen to my ramblings! But we're well over time! You may leave!'

Colette couldn't hear anything. She put her beret firmly on her head, grabbed her satchel, shoved pell-mell her books, gloves and handkerchief into it, raised her forehead up to receive Mademoiselle Lajunie's cold kiss and murmured, 'It was really interesting, I promise, but I beg your pardon, I'm late. Mum will be cross with me.'

She had seen her sweetheart. She wished for nothing more. She was only fifteen years old. Now she would have to carry away the memory of that smile, that look, along the streets, which were already growing darker, until she reached her house, until she reached the solitude of her room, until the night. She disappeared.

Mademoiselle Lajunie, her lips quivering, watched her leave. She thrust the penholder into the inkwell, as if planting it in Colette's heart. She was preparing in her head the discussion she would have as early as tomorrow with her cousin's family, the Lamberts. Methodically, relentlessly, with a kind of cold passion, she formulated it, polished it up and divided it into three main points like a French dissertation.

'Firstly, to urge them to supervise their daughter's studies; secondly, the company she keeps; thirdly, in detail, how she spends the day. To advise them: a) to remove her from her current school, the freedom it affords to her being undoubtedly a destructive influence on her; b) to enrol her as a day student in a school that I will recommend to them, and for her to have her lunch there; c) to have her accompanied when she goes out on Thursdays and Sundays. Finally, to try to make Colette herself understand how inappropriate her behaviour is.

When she had noted this down, since the room was already dark, she lifted up her head and thought, 'I should close the shutters and turn the lamp on.'

But she didn't move. It was the first evening of spring. Someone was laughing, someone was singing from the depths of those dark apartments, in the courtyard. A young maidservant, taking a momentary break from her chores, had approached the window. Motionless, her bare arms resting on the balustrade of the little balcony, she was leaning forward. She seemed to be listening to some unknown faint echo from the street or to some wild, sweet call.

Mademoiselle Lajunie sighed. The sense of her loneliness overwhelmed her. She wanted to forgive Colette for her indifference and contempt.

'She's too young, she doesn't understand,' she thought.

But she knew that wasn't the case. 'She doesn't understand any more,' she could have said. 'I came too late. Yesterday she might still have paid attention, might have been moved, but today she already has her love, her own life. A childish thing, what does it matter? He has her undivided attention. And as for me?... You search in vain, you call out in vain. There isn't a single soul to understand you. Not a single hand to reach out to you.'

It seemed to her not only that she had no support—no family, no love, no friendship (she had always known that she couldn't expect anything else)—but also that the past itself seemed dark, banal and impoverished to her. This sentimental affair between a little governess and a man older than her, a man spoilt by life. It was strange... In that faraway time she had occasionally suspected that he didn't really love her, that this was just how he was filling the few empty years between his widowhood and his second marriage. Indeed, one day, he did remarry... How many sleepless nights she had had, how many tears! But time had passed, and little by little she had rewritten patiently and tenderly in her mind the past as it should have been. She remembered now. He was fickle; he courted every woman he met; he loved his cards and wine.

But there she halted the machinery of her memory with a savage and vehement determination. For if the past were to desert her too, what would be left to her?

'Enough ramblings!' she said quietly. 'Let's think about tomorrow. The most important thing is to get the task for the day done. 'The Task for the Day'… There's a good essay title for Colette.'

Pursing her lips, she took her notepad and pen and began to cancel her classes for the coming week. For each letter the wording was the same:

> *As I am in need of a surgical procedure at short notice, I must temporarily call a halt to the mathematics (or French or history) classes given up until now to your little boy (or to your dear little girl).*

She had lit the lamp. The young boy in the opposite apartment was reading a novel hidden in a Latin dictionary and glanced occasionally at the severe face of the old teacher, who was writing unhurriedly. She reminded him of the homework to be done for tomorrow, the final-year exams, all of life's hardships. She looked up. They exchanged a cold, mistrustful glance, then each turned away without understanding the other.

MAGIC

In Finland, during the Revolution in 1918, there were a few of us, both boys and girls, who found entertainment in table-turning when evening came on. We lived in the middle of a forest. It was winter. Summer only lasts three months over there. As soon as twilight fell, the forest trails became dangerous: fugitive rebels hid behind the trees and in the snow-filled gullies, and the soldiers of the opposing army pursued them, tracking them from coppice to coppice. Gunshots were exchanged, and if a stray bullet hit a Russian traveller who had taken refuge in this land, far from his own revolution... well! We had no consul to protect us or to inform our family of an untimely death.

In this village we made up a small Russian community that subsisted somehow in an old wooden house, a derelict guesthouse comprising vast dark bedrooms and large empty drawing rooms. One of them had been reserved for the young ones; our parents played bridge or whist in the adjoining rooms.

The electricity had been cut off as early as November; we were allowed six candles per evening: four lit up the players' tables, two ours. Imagine an enormous room with low ceilings and arched windows without curtains or shutters, the panes covered with ice. There was a piano in a corner, under a grey ticking cover, a mirror in a large wooden frame on the wall, a cupboard where a few disparate Balzac volumes sat next to jam jars, (which were unfortunately mostly empty) and finally, in the middle of the room, there was a small pedestal table.

We all sat around this table; the two candles were planted in bottles. How can I describe the silence of those northern nights, which were without a breath of wind, without a screech of wheels, without a cry of joy on a pathway, without a call, without a laugh? Only the occasional light dry crack of a gunshot in the forest or the crying of a child awoken in an upstairs bedroom. Then the mother could be heard throwing down her playing cards and running towards the stairs, the swish of her long dress fading away through the corridors. Those corridors were endless, icy, sinister. We usually made sure to go up to our rooms together, all at once; we crossed the corridors in a group, laughing, singing, our hearts choked with fear.

I don't know whether it was the nervous state we were in or the carryings-on of some practical jokers, but I had never seen tables as light, as easily bridled under

Magic

our hands and flung from wall to wall, careening like a little boat in a stormy wind and in the end making such a racket that our parents would come up, begging us to find some other way to amuse ourselves. They said that the banging of that damned table and the sound of the gunshots were really more than they could take and that deference ought to be paid to old age.

We therefore modified and improved our method after a while. This is how we proceeded: we inscribed the alphabet on a sheet of paper; in the centre we placed an upturned saucer marked with a pencil line; we pressed the very tips of our fingers very lightly on the edge of the saucer and it moved from one letter to another, forming words and sentences at a tremendous speed.

None of us—for we were between fifteen and twenty years old, the age of scepticism—believed in supernatural manifestations, but we thought, with good reason, that the darkness, the silence and probably also the danger to which we were beginning to grow accustomed, but which had kept us in suspense for months, we thought that all this was enough to awaken the subconscious forces of our souls and allow us to sense more strongly and subtly than usual our desires, our inner inclinations and our dreams. Indeed, as you can imagine, love was all that interested us, and so the magic saucer ceaselessly revealed, commented upon, and spelled out our hopes and desires.

As it happened, it was the evening of 6 January. In Russia on that night the young girls go out onto their

105

doorsteps and ask passers-by for their names, and that will be the name of their as-yet unknown fiancé. Others throw burning wax in cold water and try to guess, according to the shape it takes on as it suddenly hardens, the destiny that awaits them. Crude likenesses of crosses, rings or crowns are sometimes lifted out of the water. There were many other games, but to all of them we preferred the one that had already kept us occupied for so many evenings in that icy drawing room.

It was then that one of us—let's call him Sacha—a twenty-year-old boy, asked, 'Spirit, tell me the name of the woman of my destiny.'

Sacha was courting a sturdy blonde girl called Nina, so we all expected that the spirit would obediently spell out her name, but the saucer spun quickly under our fingers and we read: Doris.

This name, while quite common in English, doesn't exist in Russian.

'Is this a joke? I heard you laugh,' Nina said somewhat nervously.

She gestured at me as well as my neighbour. We protested our good faith.

'Let's start again. Let the spirit repeat the name!'

'D-O-R-I-S,' Sacha read very quietly.

'The family name,' we demanded.

The saucer gave the letters: 'W-I-L-L-I-A-M-S.'

'You picked that name out of an English novel!' Nina exclaimed, shrugging her shoulders. 'This is stupid! Will you just admit that this is a joke?…'

Nothing could convince her. She violently pushed back her chair.

'This is idiotic! Get something else! What shall we do?'

'The mirrors?' I suggested, rather timidly since I was the youngest and merely tolerated by them.

This is another activity for the evening of 6 January. You remain alone in a dark room. You place two candles in front of a large mirror and two smaller mirrors, one to the right, the other to the left of your head. You wait. You wait for midnight to chime. The flames from the candles form a long, dark, sinuous path in the mirror. After a certain amount of time you cease to see your own pale, anxious face. Shadows emerge from the depths of the mirror and you shape them according to your dreams.

So it was arranged. We each took turns alone before our reflections; the others waited in the darkness of the corridor, huddled up against the door, telling ghost stories in whispers in order to heighten, if at all possible, the atmosphere of the evening.

When it was Sacha's turn to leave the room he seemed dumbfounded and in shock.

'I swear, I don't care what you say,' he said. 'I saw a woman's face. She was smiling. She was wearing a little black hat with roses and she made a gesture of taking off a veil or lifting a half-veil or something...'

'Did you see her face?'

'Only for a moment, and then everything disappeared

'Was she at least pretty?'

He seemed so absorbed that he didn't answer. I'll leave you to imagine the teasing that followed, which irritated Nina even more than him.

Then... time passed. A long time. Years. A handful of the Russians went back to their country and disappeared afterwards as if thrown to the bottom of the sea. Others came to Paris, among them Sacha and Nina, who had got married in Helsingfors a few months after that 6 January.

I saw them regularly. They didn't seem unhappy. Not happy either, I must say. But Russian émigrés, caught between the worry of finding work, the debts to pay and identity cards to renew, hardly have the time to contemplate their married bliss. They live together because they started that way, and little by little the years stagger on.

One day, at the home of mutual friends, I met Sacha. In the evening he saw me home. It was autumn.

'You know something? I found Doris Williams,' he said.

He didn't need to elaborate. I remembered suddenly, with an extraordinary vividness, the large, dark, bare drawing room, the mirror hung on the wall and that little old yellow fir pedestal table...

'Where?'

'At...'

He named a Russian family I knew.

'I came in,' he said. 'A woman was there and she was wearing a black hat with roses. She took out a cigarette when I came in and to light it she lifted a short black half-veil. I thought, "Where have I seen her before?" I couldn't locate that memory... I found out she was an English journalist. She was no longer very young: she must have been around forty. She told us that she had travelled a lot, and every one of the countries she knew, I had spent time there too or had passed through them in the course of my wanderings, during or after the Revolution but never at the same time as her. I was in Persia in 1919, and she was there in 1921. I was in Bournemouth for eight days three years ago, and she was there last April. Finally, we missed each other by forty-eight hours in Salzburg four years ago. As she got up to leave, all of a sudden I remembered that night in Finland and I said, "Your name is Doris Williams, isn't it?" She seemed surprised: "It was my maiden name. I'm married now." She left. I let her leave.'

'Doris Williams is a very common name,' I said to reassure him.

He made an effort to smile.

'It is, isn't it?'

'And yet,' I said, 'if...'

'I'm married,' he answered, shrugging his shoulders. 'I have children. To hell with destiny! It came too late.'

'Ah, well, if it is truly meant to be that this woman must be yours and you hers, you'll find each other again...'

'God forbid,' he muttered. 'My life is tough enough, difficult enough without adding feelings or passion to the equation.'

'You will meet her,' I said.

And yet it was he who was right. I read this morning that in London the body of a woman was found in her appartment, a journalist by trade, Doris Milne-Williams, who took her own life. It was explained that she had suffered some personal grief and that she had lived separated from her husband. Somewhere there must have been, in the threads woven for us by destiny, an error, a missing link.

THE FIRE

When haggling over an estate, she would take the money out of her handbag there and then and line up the banknotes in wads of 5,000 on the table, in front of the silent farmers. The soil is rich in our part of the world; it's difficult to part with it. You need to see the cash, feel it, hear it lightly rustle between your fingers before agreeing to give up a patch of land. This she knew. Her parents had been livestock dealers and had taught her how to lure one's prey and how to let it sense the primacy of wealth at the same time as the fairness of the terms so as to instil respect without hatred. Of Madame Georges they said, 'She dresses fancy but she doesn't talk fancy.' The Georges had been wholesale butchers in Paris, supplying meat only to the restaurants and not to the 'carnivores', as they said proudly. Now they were retired, living near us in the Count of Neuville's old house and little by little were snatching up the best of the region's fields, woods and farms. Madame Georges was short, dainty, and ladylike in her choices of dress and perfume; and of course she had received an excellent education; she read all the new novels for her own enjoyment, she was a theatregoer, she could name without error and in the correct order Sacha Guitry's wives and the recently elected members of the Académie française, and she knew the most famous faces in Paris to see. At the same time she was extraordinarily skilled in all the tasks of rural life: she made her own butter, preserves and pickles with her slender fingers, the nails of which were painted red. She rose at dawn, went to bed early to save money on the lighting, stood her ground against all the farmhands and, if necessary, threw them out of the door, not deigning to call on her husband for any help, and her shrill voice reigned supreme in the house. She was very much a strong-willed woman, and her husband feared her. He was markedly older than her, had a broad neck and heavy jowls and was short-winded. From 1914 to 1918 he had fought bravely, and on several occasions he had even shown formidable courage. He had been decorated with the Croix de Guerre and the Médaille Militaire. He had been carrying out the duties of the mayor, a position put to him some time earlier. He felt more comfortable in this position. The mayor was old and sick; his constituents had got into the habit of turning to Georges in cases of difficulty, and he enjoyed this role as a natural leader. The Georges had no children. Their sole concern was the management of their wealth. Their only dream was to accumulate more assets, and when at night Madame Georges heard her husband toss and turn and sigh next to her, she would immediately awake and, leaning towards him, say 'Are you thinking about the Jauts' farm?' or 'Is it the Saulnais' wood you want?' without ever being mistaken. They had no confidence in securities or money. What they wanted was land. That's how they began to lust after the Martins' estate.

The Martins, who were old and wealthy, would certainly not have given in, had their son, a solicitor based in Moulins, not speculated, done some bad deals and squandered his clients' money. In order to save him from ruin, his parents turned to the Georges. That's when Monsieur Georges purchased the area known locally as Montjeu from them: the farm and the hundred hectares of land on which stood a dwelling house rented to a Parisian painter. The little chateau with its pointed towers was built at the end of a canal that was once full of water but which was now dried up and covered with dead leaves. It was the eve of All Saints. The Georges had come to Montjeu to sign the deed of sale. Sitting in the car, next to her husband, who was driving, Madame Georges was calculating in hundredweights of wheat, livestock and fruit the profit she would make from the land she was about to purchase. The air was crisp; the wind was blowing down from the nearby mountains of the Auvergne, the verdant foothills of which could be seen rising up against the sky, and from their base spread a luscious, peaceful countryside. A flock of large turkeys crossed the road, blocking the car's way, then fled, gobbling frantically. Sheltered under an umbrella, a woman chased before her two large cows with white and ginger coats. The clouds, when they parted, revealed a crimson sky, and for a moment the sun glistened over the wet flanks of the animals trotting towards the cowshed, over trees still laden in places with dry pink leaves and over the round bossages sculpted on the chateau walls.

'It's pretty lavish here,' Monsieur Georges said with a smile.

From a distance they admired the building with delight, and Madame Georges sighed: if she had pushed her husband to purchase the estate, it was of course out of self-interest, but also because she was curious to get to know the tenant of the little chateau. To know someone with a famous name is of no importance. Everyone in Paris called him by his first name, Mario, with the kind of simplicity particular to a lower class of fame. But Monsieur Georges' wife had no awareness of such nuances. In her dreams she imagined the artist to be handsome, flamboyant and young; it was true that he had been all those things during the years immediately after the previous war. The spark of a name travels from Paris into the provinces slowly, often like a dead star whose beams are only seen when the radiant core itself has burnt out.

'Would you slow down! You're driving so fast!' said Madame Georges.

She leaned over the door in her fashionable red hat, her cheeks delicately powdered and her black eyes sharp and round. Her piercing gaze darted across the little chateau, inspecting each gleaming window, one after the other. 'It's badly maintained,' she said aloud with contempt. 'I wonder could he not take all those dead leaves out of the canal.' 'Maybe he finds it picturesque,' said Georges, laughing heartily.

With every gust of wind the leaves were torn from the trees and gently flew away to rest along the stone embankments. Under the force of a stronger gust, one little tree shed almost all its leaves; until then it had kept its golden finery; it was now forever stripped of it in one fell swoop; the tree remained standing, shivering and exposed, swaying in the humid air.

Georges accelerated and, leaving the chateau behind, drove towards the farm where the solicitor was waiting for them. The deed of sale was signed, after which the old Martins offered everyone a little something to eat. The kitchen was large and clean; it held a purely decorative bed; no one ever slept in it, but it was seen as visible proof of wealth, being a feather bed with a big yellow satin eiderdown and pillows in embroidered cases. Cured ham was served, together with fromage blanc, bowls of cream and small slabs of butter stamped with a sprig of holly.

'My butter is better than hers,' Madame Georges thought. She always compared whatever she ate to the produce of her own dairy or farmyard, and if ever she were to discern any kind of superiority in someone else's food, her entire day would be ruined. But this had never happened, really: the Georges were flourishing, as they say where we come from.

They drank some marc. Madame Martin placed on the table a cake that she had just taken out of the oven. She was pouring the coffee into little white, gilt-edged teacups decorated with pink daisies when the door opened to let in a newcomer.

The Martins got up and pulled forward a chair, which Madame Martin wiped with her apron.

'These are your new landlords, Monsieur,' she said, gesturing towards the Georges. 'The estate has been handed over.'

'That's the painter,' Georges whispered to his wife.

She elbowed him and murmured, 'For goodness' sake, I know.' She turned at once towards the visitor and offered him a plate, a slice of cake and a glass of marc. She was the kind of woman who cannot bear to see someone else play the part of lady of the house before her, the kind who is always ready to say 'Wait, let me do it!', who authoritatively takes charge of carving the meat and pouring out the coffee.

The painter took the cake and marc. He was a tall man and seemed even taller because he held his head backwards slightly when he spoke, as if looking with disdain upon the person to whom he was talking, either out of something like contempt or because, as a painter, he was used to contemplating his work that way. Extraordinarily handsome, with fine features and fully white hair, he had dazzling dark eyes, and his gaze fell approvingly upon Madame Georges. He clearly didn't expect to see such hands and a slender waist on a wealthy butcher. Madame Georges caught sight of the mocking smile that he wasn't even trying to hide, but far from taking any exception to it, she felt proud: 'A butcher is as good as any society woman of his,' she thought.

She cast a provocative glance in his direction and placed on the table, very near him so that he might admire it, her beautifully formed bare arm adorned with a large gold bracelet.

'It's a pleasure to meet you,' he said, lowering his voice. 'You're the one taking over from old Madame Martin then? You're the one I'll talk to about fixing my drainpipes?'

'Ah, Monsieur! The repairs are at your expense,' she said promptly, and she recited the relevant section of the lease, which she knew by heart.

'Ah!' he laughed, 'I can tell you're from the area. They're crafty around here, they're careful with their money. But you must have lived in Paris? Your hat is from Paris.'

Monsieur Georges was sipping his marc, listening to his wife and the painter. He felt neither jealousy nor even a hint of rancour at being left out of their conversation, but rather the supercilious guarantee of possession. Madame Georges was not the kind of woman to forget her duties; he knew her: she wasn't the sensuous kind. Wealth and recognition were all she wanted, and with the retired butcher she had all this and more! And so he very soon stopped thinking about his wife. He saw once again in his mind's eye those meadows, those fields that were now his. The canal should have been filled with water and populated with carp and tench. The painter had a ten-year lease on the chateau, seven of which had elapsed. In three years he would be the sole master of the estate.

He nodded assent when his wife turned to him to say: 'Monsieur is inviting us to visit the chateau.'

They took their leave of the Martins. Mario suggested walking along the path separating the chateau from the farm, but Madame Georges had a different idea: she was keen to show off her car.

They got out at the front steps. Madame Georges considered the house from a closer vantage and more avidly now. It was beautiful, not short of grandeur, but there was something intangibly sad about it. The garden was neglected, and Madame Georges searched in vain for all that brings a country home to life: dogs bounding around, poultry pecking at their grain, little goats running and playing in a field. Not a sound broke the silence here. The wind itself had fallen silent; big clouds tinted with purple and yellow were gathering over the mountains.

'It's going to rain,' said Georges. 'Getting back home won't be easy: my windscreen wipers are broken.'

'You should have had them repaired yesterday, of course, as I told you,' replied Madame Georges, who took great pleasure in speaking sharply and sternly to her husband in public.

It was her way of proving to the world her authority and the high esteem in which her husband held her.

Monsieur Georges winked in Mario's direction as if meaning to say that, according to the well-known proverb, one should listen to a woman but not answer her.

'You'll sleep here,' said Mario, taking Madame Georges by the arm in an overly familiar way.

'You're joking,' she replied with a sharp laugh, 'but that's what we do in the countryside. You come to have something to eat and you stay till the following morning. That wouldn't be an issue where we live: we have eleven beds,' she said proudly.

'Ten too many for me,' he murmured in her ear.

The finest men can sometimes take great pleasure in showing themselves to be crude, and here is why the mysterious charm of certain women works on them: with such women, the mind is allowed to drop to its lowest point; the result is a vague but exquisite sense of peace.

They entered the house. Georges quickly noticed that the furniture was luxurious: lots of divans, carpets and paintings. In the studio there wasn't one free inch of space on the walls: they were covered with paintings and tapestries. 'They can't have cost him much,' Georges thought. 'Probably his own and his friends'.'

For this reason he looked upon them with contempt: everything he owned in his house had been bought and paid for upfront. The room was cold and had the same air of sadness as the rest of the house. Madame Georges looked uneasily at the portraits' hollow eyes.

'It's like an art gallery,' she said.

Mario lit the lamps that shed light on some of the canvasses.

'The portrait of the Countess of Noailles,' he said. 'It dates back to 1910. This one's more recent: it's Princess B. in her infanta costume, the one she wore to the Zameths' ball three years ago, and here's Alexandre Adam, the musician.'

Madame Georges was following him. She listened to him utter all these famous names with intense curiosity and a kind of jealous regret: until now she had always thought of herself according to what she inspired in others. She was one of the happiest, the most privileged, the wealthiest, the most fulfilled people in our town, and to her own mind, with her gold, her land, her farm animals, her splendid dairy cows, she saw herself as queen of the land, soaring over the small farming and shopkeeping classes at inaccessible heights. She looked down on the aristocrats, whose estates were little by little falling into her hands. But here she had a brief glimpse of a world unknown to her, shining very far from her reach, with strange, pale reflections, just as a denizen of this earth can see the pearlescent moon shed its mysterious light over the horizon.

'Do you not get bored in this solitude? Do you spend the winter here?' she asked.

'Oh, no! Only the autumn months. October and November.'

'That's odd. That's the most tedious time of year in the countryside,' said Georges, who was absent-mindedly flicking through a book on the table. He read aloud the title: *The Possessed* by Dostoevsky. 'You read a lot,' he concluded, a note of sadness in his voice, as if he had discovered in his host some new flaw.

'But it's around this time I enjoy the countryside!' Mario exclaimed. 'It's humid and mild; it smells of apple and woodsmoke. I'm perfectly happy here with my brushes, my music, my books.'

'Ah,' George sighed, 'you play music as well!'

'In that room,' Mario said, 'only beautiful and rare things are allowed. I can hide myself away in there much better than in Paris. Here I can ignore all the hideousness of the modern world. I probably seem old-fangled to you, vieux jeu,' he said with a hint of bitterness in his voice that Madame Georges couldn't detect.

And how could she? She knew nothing of that life, that ageing glory, that desperate love of a beauty which was no longer in fashion and which made young people sneer. She didn't understand that everything in Paris was a source of pain for him: the memory of his achievements, the triumph of his rivals, the blame, even the praise.

'I'm from another time, Madame,' he continued. 'I'm a contemporary of Pierre Louÿs, of D'Annunzio, of all those who lived only for, and by, beauty. Women, for instance… no one loves women any more. I for one am not ashamed to admit that a well-rounded leg, a beautiful hand, a perfect body drives me wild. It's very curious, you know: in novels nowadays you'll notice that the heroine is never beautiful. Pretty, yes, attractive, yes, but beauty, true, immortal beauty doesn't move anyone, doesn't interest anyone any more. And as for me, I've no interest in the passions of the mob: politics, the fate of couples... That's all rubbish, Madame, rubbish. I'm old. I'm vain enough to tell you that before you figure it out for yourself. I can speak about my life in the past tense. That's my consolation prize, my revenge for having to consider that no youth'—there was such deep-rooted hatred in his voice as he uttered that word!—'will ever know a life like mine. To not allow into one's home or into one's life the smallest atom of ugliness, what strength, what balance that asks of an artist! I'm an artist. Today's artists are hacks or speculators. I alone, together with a few overlooked friends like me, old like me, we keep that worship of eternal beauty in our hearts.'

Madame Georges didn't expect a painter to express himself like a butcher, of course; nonetheless, this impassioned outburst came as something of a surprise to her. Mario's eyes were shining with a strange brightness. His voice was strident and harsh. He suddenly turned off the lamps.

'I'm an old owl. I live in darkness. Eyes accustomed to shadow develop an exquisite sharpness of perception. For instance, look how dead leaves take on beautiful, strange tones in twilight. See, this one is the colour of a scabious.'

'I don't see anything,' said Georges, opening his eyes wide, but to no avail.

Mario smiled with a sad loftiness.

'Really? I'm not surprised.'

He spun on his heels and led them out of the studio to a small neighbouring sitting room. He sat down between them on the divan, and all of a sudden his face and attitude changed; he was once again down-to-earth and friendly; he spoke to Georges about the area and its inhabitants. At the same time, in the dark, he was pinching Madame Georges' thigh. 'He must have been with many women...' she thought.

At times, however, Georges fell silent, not knowing quite what to say, and in the sudden silence Mario's face grew still and attentive, as if he had detected some distant sound that didn't reach anyone else's ears. 'Do you hear something?' Madame Georges couldn't help asking him.

He turned briskly to her.

'There are rats in the attic. Do you not hear anything?'

She listened. The silence was heavy and deep; raindrops were rolling down the windowpanes. She shivered.

'I'd have dark thoughts if I had to live here.'

'I have books and papers piled up in the attic,' Mario said. 'I had vague ideas about writing my memoirs one day but I got tired of that project like many others. Sometimes, at night, when I can't sleep, I amuse myself by going up there and rereading some old letters. There's a litter of white rats that are barely afraid of me any more. I bet you never suffer from insomnia,' he said, addressing Georges. 'Oh, lucky you!'

He then set about taking them for a tour of the house. In one bedroom Madame Georges caught sight of a portrait of a very beautiful woman dressed in the fashion of thirty years ago, an ostrich feather boa around her neck, and on her head one of those large hats they called a mob cap, trimmed with sheer black mousseline frills.

'My wife,' Mario said.

'Ah! I didn't realise,' Georges said.

'Yes, I'm a widower.'

'Do you not have any children?' asked Georges, who felt growing unease overcome him: the very atmosphere of the house, its rooms cluttered with furniture, the musky smell rising imperceptibly from the old hangings on the walls, the painter's conversation, of which Georges only understood every other sentence, all this stupefied him slightly. He yawned several times behind his hand.

'Do you not have any children?' he repeated automatically.

'No.'

'That's a pity,' Georges said distractedly.

'My wife died giving birth, and the child didn't survive.'

He turned away, opened the door, invited the Georges to go before him, and all three found themselves once again in the studio. It was late, Georges signalled discreetly to his wife by pointing at the time on a clock face and calling her attention to the night that was thickening outside. Madame Georges pretended not to notice.

Eventually her husband could no longer take it. He got up resolutely.

'Goodnight, Monsieur. It's been a privilege. Julie, it's time to go home. Perhaps we shall see each other again? Of course we will… I mean…'

'Would you give me the pleasure of your company for lunch this Sunday?' Mario asked. 'You enjoy your food, Madame Georges: a pretty woman should always enjoy her food. I have an old cook here, my only housemaid, incidentally, with a young lad about fifteen years old who helps with the housework. She's as deaf as a post. She's been in my service for thirty years. But she has the gift, the genius of fine cuisine. She'll make us a salmi of woodcock that you'll enjoy.'

'Certainly. That would be lovely. We're very honoured, very flattered,' Georges repeated.

They took their leave of Mario. In the car, both were silent. Julie was observing her husband out of the corner of her eye to see if he had noticed how she had been cajoling Mario: he had kept very close to her on the little divan and in the studio. What a man! She had never seen the like of him. He wasn't young, that much was true, but such grace, such arrogance! He had fine bronzed hands, clean, soft and expressive like lips.

'What are you making for us for dinner tonight, Julie?' Georges asked.

'Ah, I don't know,' she answered irritably. 'You'll find out.'

She couldn't see him in the dark. She could hear his

hoarse breathing, which got on her nerves to the point that she raised her voice.

'You eat too much anyway. It's disgusting how big you are! You can hardly breathe.'

'All right, all right, you've made your point,' he grumbled.

'It's curious,' she thought, 'I can usually put up with him, but as soon as another man excites me… I can no longer stand poor Georges. That's the way it's always been.'

Madame Georges was no paragon of virtue. Since she had been living in the countryside, occasions of sin had been rare, and besides, her instinct for ownership had little by little stifled every other instinct in her. However, when she lived in Paris… She closed her eyes and sighed. Never had she met anyone like Mario. She began to construct a long romance in her head. She continued it in the evening, during the night, as she lay next to Georges, who was snoring. Only the following day, as if she had awoken from a dream, did she see the danger in such an affair.

'Ah well. He'll sleep with me once and ditch me afterwards,' she thought bluntly. 'No, no, I won't have it said that Julie Georges has lost her head, at her age, like a schoolgirl.'

She was a bourgeoise, tortured by a thirst for recognition. The thought that a lover might one day make a fool of her, mock her manners, the company she kept or the books she read was more than she could bear. Everyone in his own place, everyone among his own kind. She had nothing in common with the famous painter.

She pretended to have the flu so as not to have to go to the chateau the following Sunday. Mario didn't renew his invitation. She continued to busy herself with her cows and her hens, counting her money, and in her harshness was now something simultaneously bitter and fortifying, like a tonic. Monsieur Georges and the maid suffered a lot from her mood.

One day, at the end of November, the Martins' 'hand' (where we come from that's what we call the workers on the farms), out of breath, ran into Monsieur Georges' kitchen. The Martins remained as sharecroppers on their former estate. Their hand was a tall and nimble eighteen-year-old boy, with an upturned nose and dark eyes. He asked to speak to Georges.

'There's been a fire at the chateau,' he said suddenly. 'Broke out early this afternoon. I was told to let you know.'

'Is there any damage?' asked Georges, thinking of the insurance.

'Quite a bit. But it didn't reach the stable or the grounds of the estate. Only the gentleman's furniture was ruined, and then, by God, the man himself got into trouble.'

'Trouble? What do you mean?'

The boy emptied the glass of wine that the maid had poured him, wiped his mouth and finished: 'He fell down the stairs, the smoke suffocated him.'

'He's dead?' Julie cried.

'He sure is,' the boy said indifferently.

'Good G...' Georges said.

His soul was torn with violent and conflicting feelings: the horror of such a brutal end, and the joy of becoming sole master of the estate even before the lease for the chateau had expired.

'We have to go there to see what's happened,' he said.

The car was brought to the front of the house and he got in with Madame Georges and the hand. The fire must have been smouldering in the attic since the previous day. The painter often spent the night there, as he had told them, and stray ash from his cigarette could have spread the fire to the books piled up higgledy-piggledy on the floor and to the bundles of letters.

Julie clung very tightly to her bag with both hands and was silent, her face pale and her lips pursed.

'Did you know the painter well?' the hand asked. 'He was a queer fellow, that one!'

'A queer fellow? What do you mean?'

The boy gestured vaguely with his hand.

He lived a funny kind of life, eh! What's more, we found him...' He laughed silently.

'I won't say. It can be a surprise. People were stunned, but as for me... I'd seen them... Only I didn't say a word because it's none of my business, is it?'

'For heaven's sake, what is?' Madame Georges cried.

'You'll see,' was all he answered. He leaned back, crossing his arms, a smile playing on his lips.

When they arrived at the chateau, there was still

smoke coming from the attic. Some items of furniture had been hastily taken out during the fire: a couch and three delicate little chairs had been thrown over the front steps of the chateau. The sun was setting. It had been a cold, bright day. The gathering dusk brought a chill to the air; a frosty haze was rising from the meadows, which were still green. In front of the open door a small group of men was waiting. Georges recognised the gendarmes, the Martins, the mayor and a few curious onlookers.

'From what the maid says, there would seem to be serious damage,' one of them said. 'There were small paintings like this'—he demonstrated with both hands—'which cost about 50 or 100,000 francs. But you can't really tell with her: she's deaf. You ask her one thing and she answers another.'

'Imagine! A little more wind and it would have blown to our house,' Madame Martin said. 'Accidents don't wait around to happen.'

'And what about him? The gentleman? Where is he?' asked Georges, lowering his voice.

'He was carried into his room,' the mayor answered. 'Dr Godet came, but there was nothing he could do at that stage. He's left. Would you like to come in, Madame?'

He let the landlady in before him, pointing to the door behind which lay the dead body.

'Is he alone?' Madame Georges asked as she paused over the threshold.

The mayor, an old countryman in a black smock,

slowly took off his hat and turned it for a moment between his hands.

'Alone? No, he's not alone. Go ahead, Madame. There's a maid with him and...'

He didn't finish. Madame Georges took two steps and paused. The body was laid out on a bed. He had been dressed in a purple dressing gown. With his long bare neck, his rigid white chin pointing upwards, his large eyes closed and that nose, whose shape death had altered (for Madame Georges didn't remember it being so long, so pale and so stiff), he seemed unrecognisable. He looked old and fragile. A woman was kneeling at his side.

'The maid,' Madame Georges thought.

She took another step and suddenly recoiled. In the shadow of the bed she had just discovered two shapes that she initially took for two children. They were the size of boys of six or eight years of age. When she approached them they turned their faces to her, and then she saw that they were not children, but two dwarves. They had stocky chests, heavy square shoulders, but very small legs. They had the faces of grown men, with long deep wrinkles, and their eyes had the sad, inscrutable, and in some way more than human look of certain incurable invalids in hospices. They got up and took each other by the hand. What heightened the awe and pity they inspired was their perfect resemblance. They remained silent, and Madame Georges too was mute. The old woman, who had not heard her come in and who was still praying, her face hidden, did not lift up her head.

'Do you live here?' Madame Georges asked.

But they didn't answer. They didn't seem stupid, but fearful like wild animals. Then, burning with curiosity, she tapped the maid on the shoulder.

'Who are these… these gentlemen?' she asked.

'Yes, it's a terrible tragedy,' the deaf woman answered in a sharp, monotonous voice, as if intoning a liturgical chant. 'I've been in his service for more than thirty years. I'm the one who looked after his lady in her last moments, and I didn't expect to ever see him like this, but, as they say, "No one knows who lives and who dies."'

'Yes, I know, I know,' Madame Georges said, 'but I'm asking you who these are? Who are these two?'

She indicated the two motionless dwarves with a gesture and a glance.

The old woman finally understood or guessed the question.

'His sons,' she said.

'These are his sons? They can't be! Where on earth did they live? Were they hidden away? He never told a soul about them! He was ashamed of them, was that it? Are they his legitimate sons? His heirs?' Madame Georges asked, and without regard for the dead she was shouting in the deaf woman's ear.

But the woman could or would say nothing more. Madame Georges could not get another word out of her. At that moment two nuns, who had been sent for and to keep vigil over the dead, entered the bedroom. Madame Georges left.

Two days later Mario was buried. The two dwarves were the chief mourners. They were the painter's legitimate sons, his sole heirs. For nearly thirty years he had managed to keep them in his house, under his roof, without anyone suspecting that they were his children; very few people knew that they existed at all. They had been spotted during his travels. They had been mistaken for domestics, for monstrous buffoons sheltered and kept on a whim. Now they were walking behind the coffin, their small faces sad, pale and weary. The hearse was covered with splendid flowers. The farmers looked at them, nodded and said, 'That cost a good deal,' and 'That wasn't cheap.' The contrast between this pomp, the beauty of the flowers and the look of the two poor dwarves was so strange, so striking that the Georges themselves were filled with emotion and remained silent. At times it seemed to them that at the heart of this scene was some kind of deeper meaning, some mystery that they could not grasp.

THE SPELL

The power of childhood memories lies in their share of mystery. Events and characters from the past can seem like cabinets with secret doors: you think you know them but you realise years later that you were wrong. What once seemed simple is now cloaked in shadows and secrecy. By contrast, what intrigued you then is now reduced to petty tales of inheritance and adultery. Childhood ignorance and forgetfulness thus form a world that's only half revealed and that remains half veiled. For this reason, perhaps, it remains in the memory with such vivid colours.

When I was eight, there lived in the Ukrainian town where I was born a family that I often visited with my young aunt. The father had retired from the army. I've forgotten his rank and name but I can still see the house, the furniture and the faces.

Their home was far from ours; we lived in the middle of the town, they in the surrounding areas. To get there was almost a voyage. I remember the old brown walls, the rust-gnawed iron roofs and an infinite number of drainpipes. It was a spring day the first time I went there. The snow was melting and flowing like silver as it made a lively, cheerful sound, surrounding the house with its glistening gushes and rapid whisperings, running along the street. I went inside. I felt shy and had to be dragged along. A little girl took my hand. Her name was Nina. She would later become my friend. I was standing in the hall as my aunt loosened the shawls and collars that protected me from the cold. The little girl was looking at me with a smile; her mouth was large, her eyes black.

'Go into the nursery,' said my aunt, who was eager to be left alone with Nina's sister to talk about their sweethearts.

My aunt and this girl were both twenty years old. My aunt was pretty. She had soft skin, a slender waist and no more wit than a chirping bird. Nina's sister was a tall girl, pale and thin. Her sharp features cut a fine silhouette, and her green eyes were so beautiful with their almond shape and grass-green colour that one couldn't help gazing into them. Nina brought me through the drawing room. I had never seen such an old house. There were a great many rooms, all very small. To pass from one to another we went up and down uneven steps made of bricks, which were often loose and shaky. It was great fun. Disorder, dereliction and neglect were everywhere to be seen, yet at the same time it was the warmest, liveliest house I'd ever seen. There was dust, spiderwebs, rickety little seats and bulging antique chests in every corner. The house smelt of strong tobacco, damp fur and mould because it was humid. The nursery walls were grey and sweating.

'Are you not worried about Nina's health?' said Mademoiselle, my nanny.

My friend's mother shrugged her soft, heavy shoulders.

'No. What can you do? The children are in good form. It's God who gives us good health and God who takes it away, Mademoiselle.'

It was certainly true that Nina was never sick. She ran barefoot on the cold wooden floors and the wet ground of the garden, she ate whatever she wanted, she went to bed after midnight, but she was beautiful and strong. I sometimes happened to stay for one or two days in that house: it rained, and I risked catching a cold on my way back home at night, when the wind blew, presaging a storm. For me and my aunt any excuse would do; I was happy to fake a sore throat or tiredness if necessary. It was wonderful to stay there! I slept in Nina's bedroom. We got up at dawn, we ran through the sleeping house and gave ourselves a quick wash or none at all. When the grown-ups weren't playing cards or sleeping, they were tidying. Visitors appeared at all hours: for morning coffee, for dinner, supper, evening tea, at midnight, whenever. Friends slept on the sofas. At around noon you would meet boys with dishevelled hair roaming the corridors in their nightclothes, introducing themselves by saying, 'I'm a friend of your son's.'

'Good morning, you're welcome' would be the answer.

The table was never cleared; the kitchen was equipped with dishes that were as heavy as rocks but of excellent quality. Certain guests would be finishing their dessert while others were only starting on their soup. The barefoot servants were constantly running from the dining room to the pantry, bringing dishes in and out. Then someone would suddenly exclaim, 'I wouldn't mind something sweet…'

'That can easily be arranged,' the lady of the house would reply affably, and again the cakes would appear, then an omelette, a cup of cocoa, some milk for the children. 'Another bowl of borscht?' And they would begin to eat again amid cigar smoke, while in the same room a game of whist was being played and the sounds of both a piano and a violin would come in from the adjoining drawing room.

'Goodness, do they not ever work?' said Mademoiselle, who, being a foreigner, had some rather particular ideas about life.

But these Russians expected their daily bread from the Tsar, from their land, from God. He made them rich and poor just as he gave them good health and sickness. What use was there in worrying?

Sofia Andreïevna, my friend's mother, seemed old to me; she couldn't have been older than forty but she didn't wear make-up or a corset; she was stout, blonde, faded, soft and white like cream, and when she drew me into her to kiss my cheeks and say hello, I could breathe in from her neck a perfume that reminded me of fine pastries: a combination of orange blossom, vanilla and sugar.

The father was very tall and thin, but perhaps because of his size, I can't remember his features. I would have had to lean my head back to see him properly; I didn't find him interesting enough to make the effort. He lived rather apart from his family, often having his meals brought on a tray to his room. When he bumped into me he patted me on the cheek with his big cold hand. The grown-ups told me one day that he had known Chekhov very well; I don't know why I still remember that. On the father's table was a little box containing letters from the writer. He had ordered that they be burnt after his death. He was ill and knew his days were coming to an end. For this reason he had retired.

'Why burn the Chekhov letters? They belong to posterity,' said a young man in front of me had said.

The father had looked at him sombrely.

'All they want is to ride roughshod over his soul. No, all that's precious must be kept secret.'

In that house lived friends, poor relatives and old governesses; a student had come there ten years previously to make Lola—that was the name of my friend's eldest sister—and Nina's brothers work. He was supposed to stay for a month: he had never left and was still a student. He didn't have a room; the old house, vast as it was, was full. He had been sleeping on two chairs in the hall for ten years, and that didn't surprise anyone.

Near the samovar, the second seat, next to the

lady of the house, was reserved for a certain Klavdia Alexandrovna, a childhood friend of Sofia Andreïevna's. In my eyes, she was a pale, ageless woman, but one day I saw her dressing her hair. We were in the garden.

'In this house,' Mademoiselle said, 'they sleep in the drawing room but eat in the bedroom and wash themselves on the front steps.'

On stormy days rainwater was collected in tubs, and all the women of the house washed their hair outdoors and then dried it in the sun; this is how I saw Klavdia Alexandrovna's hair. It was a cloak of gold. I remained motionless, gazing in admiration at it. Her hair fell to her knees, its radiant colour shimmering in the light. Sofia Andreïevna was there too, half stretched out on a straw lounger. She was wearing a lilac dressing gown, open slightly on her heavy milk-white chest. She caught me looking and started laughing. Her chin quivered slightly when she laughed and she had a kindly, gentle, wise expression.

'If you had seen her twenty years ago,' she said to me, pointing at her friend, 'she was a young girl then; she used to let her hair down in two big golden plaits, and if she leant her head back a little, she could hold them down with her heels.'

She sighed and turned to Mademoiselle.

'Life is simpler than you think. When we were young, me and Klavdia, we loved the same man, and let me tell you, he was fond of her because of her hair and her pretty face. Only, well, she had no dowry. What can you do if God isn't inclined to bless you with wealth?

The young man's parents didn't want to hear about the marriage. There were quarrels and tears; the mother came to see Klavdia and told her, "Make my son happy. Step aside. Sacrifice yourself." She appealed to the good nature of this girl whom she had raised. In vain. Then she called the three of us one night, told us she was dying and ordered her son to marry me and Klavdia to renounce that love, but she made both of us swear before God that we would never abandon the orphan, that she would live under our roof. And that's how things ended up. I married the young man. You know him: he's my husband. We've kept the oath we made to that woman on her deathbed, and Klavdia has found her home here with us.'

I saw Klavdia Alexandrovna turn to her friend. Tears were rolling down her face. She wiped them away.

'You're my benefactress, Sonia. You know I'd give my all for you and your children. I've had the happiest life. What would I have become without you? Without shelter, without bread, perhaps doomed to teach lessons to make a living! Ah! One day I'd like to repay the debt of kindness I owe you.'

Both were crying now, and Klavdia took Sofia's hand and kissed it. Sofia drew Klavdia to her, kissed her cheeks and traced the sign of the cross on her forehead.

'God bless you! You help me around the house.'

Indeed, when cakes were brought to the table, Sofia Andreïevna, with a deep sigh, took the silver knife and plunged it down the middle of the creamy top, but then the effort seemed too great for her, and she pushed the plate towards Klavdia, who completed the task.

'Eat up,' she said to the guests. 'You haven't eaten anything yet. Come on, eat up...'

And when they helped themselves she added, 'Bless you.' Just as when someone sneezes. It's the Russian way.

Klavdia Alexandrovna had other talents. She could tell your fortune. She knew all sorts of superstitions and strange rituals... On the eve of Epiphany she slipped mirrors under the young girls' pillows: in their dreams these mirrors would show the man each would love. That same night she was to lock herself into a room with Lola and my aunt, and they would throw burning wax into a basin of water. The wax would roughly take the form of rings, crowns, roubles and crosses that would predict the future. Sometimes she taught them to turn tables; a saucer was placed on a sheet of paper covered with letters, signs and numbers. You placed your fingertips on the edge of the saucer and it ran around the table, forming words and sentences, at times sliding so fast that it had to be held back with both hands so that it wouldn't fall to the floor. Nina and I (the little ones) sat in on these sessions, and I could never find out their secret. Klavdia recited incantations, those which, according to her, addressed the dead and those which drove away thunder. I wonder to what extent she believed in it herself, but in the end, in our eyes, she had enveloped herself in a sort of mysterious charm. She was respected; young people were drawn to her. At her age, and owing to her status as someone else's poor, dependent relative, she might have been looked down on, but she wasn't: without Klavdia there was no joy.

'She knows a spell to attract love,' Lola said to my aunt.

'She knows a spell to attract love,' little Nina repeated, mimicking the grown-ups, even though as an eight-year-old she didn't have much interest in love.

I, who had been spared from the fantastical by a half-French education, was the only one to answer with scepticism.

'Is that so! If she really has the secret to love, then why isn't she married?'

How many times had the young girls tried to cajole Klavdia into revealing to them the secret of the spell, I'll leave you to guess. But she shook her head.

'Later, my sweets, later.'

It was winter. The garden was buried under a heavy snow. A lit lantern on the front steps illuminated the low white branches of the softly gleaming trees.

The dogs came in, covered in snow. In the drawing room there were card games, tea and music. I remember a pedestal lamp on a bronze stand with its red lampshade. Klavdia was drawing the cards, a large silk shawl decorated with a fringe over her shoulders. The shawl was nearly the same colour as the lampshade, and to my eyes, which were burning because of a lack of sleep—for at home I wasn't used to going to bed so late—the drawing room eventually became a dark, slightly frightening place, where two flames were burning. I fell half asleep, then woke up and started surreptitiously playing with the crimson silk, holding it up between my eyes and the light. The room took on a wonderful colour of raspberry and wine!

Meanwhile, Klavdia was murmuring quietly while shuffling the cards.

'What's in the mind, what's in the heart, what happens in the house, what's passed and what is yet to come...'

Another familiar figure in the house was the one we called the doctor, a slim blonde man with a face adorned with a short, pointy red beard that he stroked absentmindedly and dreamily. His eyes had a singular, alluring expression: his almond-shaped eyelids were always slightly lowered, a look that was simultaneously pensive, sarcastic and sad.

I wonder when he visited his patients. He could be seen in my friends' house at all hours of the day and night. We even saw him considerably more often than the master of the house, whose seat at the table often remained empty. Nina called the doctor 'Uncle', 'Uncle Serge', even though there was no family connection between them—I knew as much—but he was an old friend of the family, and besides, Russian children called the grown-ups they met at their parents' house 'Uncle' and 'Aunt'. Indeed the constant presence of the doctor at Sofia Andreïevna's side, their long conversations, their silences, nothing would have seemed suspicious to me were it not for my young aunt's stifled giggle when she alluded to it, or Mademoiselle furrowing her brow, pointing discreetly in my direction with her chin.

'Come on, shush, don't be ridiculous.'

Poor Mademoiselle! She simultaneously felt curious, scandalised and above all astonished: to her eyes, this middle-aged woman shuffling around all day in her loose dressing gown, and that courteous, quiet man, absorbed in his reveries, were not a hero and heroine fit for a love affair. And besides, the husband was so obviously aware of everything and so accepting! Ah! The bachelor flats of Paris, the evening trysts and all that airy and resplendent backdrop of courtly love! Mademoiselle, the most virtuous of women, searched for the descriptions of such love in Paul Bourget's novels, as exiles listen to the songs of their native country. These people and this great land of Russia were wild. In any case I think she and my aunt were mistaken and that the doctor and Sofia Andreïevna never had an affair. True enough, these people were wild. Out of lethargy, perhaps, or out of realism, or a frosty disposition, or for other reasons, they could be perfectly happy with platonic love. It was nonetheless clear that there was some love between Sofia Andreïevna and the doctor. Even I as a child, once my attention was aroused, could recognise it. Sofia Andreïevna's voice would break and become sharper and more tremulous when she caught sight of the Doctor. The Russian custom in the provinces was to kiss the lady of the house on the hand after the meal, and she in turn would lightly press her lips to the head of the man leaning forward. When the Doctor approached Sofia Andreïevna she looked at him... Oh! I can't describe that look in her eyes... An ineffable tenderness mixed with a regret that I could sense without understanding it, but she didn't kiss him. She smiled and he withdrew from her. My aunt observed this little game with much curiosity, whereas Lola didn't seem to notice a thing; her magnificent green eyes were bright and indifferent.

Winter passed, giving way to spring. Spring is so beautiful in that country! The streets were lined with gardens and the air smelt of lime blossom and lilac, while a gentle humidity rose up from all the lawns and from the trees pressing against one another, spreading their sugar-sweet aroma into the evening. The sunlight was slowly fading. The heat was torrid on the open squares. Thunderstorms were frequent in May. It was such a joy to run around in the wet garden afterwards! Nina would take off her shoes and stockings and stamp on the soaking grass with her bare feet. We would shake the mock orange branches and the water would rain down from them in bursts over our hair.

Sometimes the thunder struck in the evening. Then we would run down the front steps to see those sulphur-yellow lightning bolts suddenly illuminate the garden. One time we found ourselves on the threshold of the drawing room in the semi-darkness. The rain had stopped, but you could still hear the gentle rumbling of thunder fading away, rolling away towards the Dniepr.

'Klavdia Alexandrovna,' I heard my aunt say to Klavdia, 'didn't you say that the spell works the night after a storm in May?'

The young men and women there surrounded Klavdia, laughing and coaxing her. Sofia Andreïevna was still in the drawing room, but the doctor had followed us.

'The moon still has to appear,' Lola declared. 'Look! There it is.'

A beam of moonlight was slipping through the clouds.

'We also need a river or a spring,' Klavdia said.

'There's a brook at the back of the garden!' someone exclaimed.

'But it always runs dry.'

'Not after a storm like that.'

'Well...' Klavdia Alexandrovna began...

They didn't let her finish. They all dragged her away, while we, the little ones, naturally hurried after them, shrieking.

In the garden the darkness was deep. We slid on the wet grass; we held onto the tree trunks; the girls were laughing. The brook was flowing in a clearing. The clouds alternately obscured and revealed the moon.

'You must wait for it to shine at its brightest,' Klavdia said.

She knelt down by the brook's edge. I was right beside her. I looked at her with curiosity. Her face was troubled and worried and her nose twitched. She was probably caught up in her own game.

'Look, little ones, this is the spell,' she said as the last clouds were scattering and the moonlight, which appeared green, floated gently around us. 'Watch carefully.'

She removed from her finger a small ring that she always wore, and which I had often seen. It was modest:

a silver circle decorated with a dark red stone from the Caucasus. She turned it in such a way that a moonbeam struck it, suddenly scattering flashes of faint light from the stone. She hesitated for a moment, then murmured a few words that I didn't hear, and three times she swiftly plunged the ring into the brook, breaking three times the reflection of the moonlight. A little frog crouching in the grass croaked and others answered. I saw Lola suddenly start.

'Oh! those frogs, the sound they make… They gave me a fright. Is that your spell, Klavdia? Give me the ring, it's my turn, I want to try it. What are the words?'

Klavdia whispered something in her ear. Lola took the ring, repeating the incantation, so quietly at first that nobody could hear her, then, giving in to my aunt's pleading, she repeated out loud:

> *Lime blossoms, wild oat and black mandrake*
> *Three times, three times, three times,*
> *Joy, I refuse you,*
> *Innocent happiness, I refuse you,*
> *May blind passion bind me forever to…*

She paused.

'To whom?' she asked Klavdia with a laugh.

'Oh! to whomever you like,' Klavdia Alexandrovna answered in a strange, cold tone of voice. 'You know it's only a joke. Pick anyone. The one you can't love, for example, the Doctor.'

She fell silent. Everyone fell silent, holding their breath.

The Doctor suddenly threw the cigarette he was holding into the water.

'What are you doing here?' Klavdia cried out sharply through tears. 'The spell was missing the fire. Water, fire, moonlight, the three crucial elements. Finish the incantation, Lola!'

After a moment's silence the girl's voice rose again.

'May blind passion bind me forever to Serge.'

'Go to him and put the ring on his finger,' Klavdia ordered.

Serge gently pushed her away.

'Leave me alone, Lola.'

But Nina and I, as if possessed by the Devil, were dancing around the two of them.

'Please, please, Uncle Serge, let her put the ring on your finger. Are you afraid of the spell? Are you afraid of witchcraft, Uncle Serge?'

He shrugged his shoulders and offered his hand. The ring was naturally too small. Lola managed nonetheless to slide it on as far as the middle knuckle of his fourth finger, and the Doctor pulled it off immediately as if a flame had burnt him.

'Oh, give it to me now! Let me have my turn,' my aunt exclaimed.

'There's no point,' Klavdia answered lifelessly. 'The spell only works once.'

After that scene she refused to participate in any kind of magic game any more. We hadn't forgotten the incantation, however, and ten times a day Nina and I plunged a ring made of braided blades of grass in the brook, repeating through hysterical laughter, 'Lime blossoms, wild oat and black mandrake…'

Then: 'May blind passion bind me forever to…'

And we would end with the most unlikely names: old Stépan, the *dvornik*; Ivan Ivanitch, my mathematics teacher; or Jouk, the black dog.

One day, however, Lola overheard us. She lunged at us and grabbed Nina by the shoulders.

'I forbid you to do that, do you hear me, you little brat! I won't… allow it.'

She was stammering. Her face was convulsed. She pulled her sister by the ear and burst into sobs. Nina fell silent, wide-eyed with astonishment.

'Is she crazy?' she asked me once Lola had fled. 'What's wrong with her?'

I didn't know. I suggested a game of hide-and-seek.

Time passed. I can't remember whether two or six months or more had passed. One evening we were in need of some rags from which to cut dolls' dresses. We usually got them from Klavdia Alexandrovna. I ran into her bedroom. She was standing by the window, her hands crossed over her chest, and was looking at the dark garden. The lamps were not lit. On the sofa I saw Lola and Uncle Serge. They were sitting next to each other; they didn't speak. Lola was moving her hand repetitively; she was brushing back a loose strand of hair that kept falling over her eyes.

Catching sight of me, Klavdia Alexandrovna suddenly turned mad with anger; she had sudden inexplicable fits of rage.

'What are you coming in here for? Go away!' she shouted, stamping her foot. 'Who comes into a bedroom without knocking?'

As a matter of fact, I had tapped at the door, but they hadn't heard me. I tried to say as much, but Lola had stood up.

'Leave her alone, Klavdia,' she said.

She lit the lamp. I noticed there was a slight stagger in her step like when one is awoken suddenly in the middle of the night. On her bare neck was a red mark. I noted it carefully: it looked like a bite mark. However, for fear of being scolded again, I said nothing and skulked away. Behind me the key turned violently in the lock.

After that I have no memory until the evening when we were all gathered as usual in the drawing room. Sofia Andreïevna, Uncle Serge and other friends were playing cards, while Klavdia, sitting at the piano, made me and Nina practise a piano four-hands piece. The door opened and Lola appeared. She was so pale! She crossed the drawing room, then stopped in front of the players' table and looked at them silently for a few moments.

'I'm going to a friend's house,' she eventually said to her mother.

It was nine in the evening. Her mother raised no objection, didn't enquire as to the friend's name or when her daughter would be back. As I said, in that house everyone lived as they pleased.

'Well,' she answered calmly, 'God bless you.'

These simple words—the expression is commonplace

in Russian—made nonetheless an extraordinary impression on Lola. She interlocked and unlocked her fingers vigorously. She looked at all of us anxiously. No one noticed a thing. The piano piece for four-hands had come to an end. Klavdia played a few bars of 'The Happy Farmer', then, with no transition, a melody so sweet and so sensuous that it made you feel like crying, laughing, hiding in a dark corner and staying there motionless for the whole night, listening. Lola left the room. A little later Uncle Serge threw down his cards.

'I have a patient to visit tonight,' he said.

He bowed before Sofia Andreïevna, kept for a long time the hand she held out to him pressed against his lips and then also left the house. Klavdia Alexandrovna stopped playing and disappeared into her bedroom.

Uncle Serge's departure had disturbed the whist players. Sofia Andreïevna soon found herself alone and began a game of patience. Mademoiselle, sitting very straight in an armchair opposite her, wearing her austere black dress, her little white collar and her golden chain which hung low over her small chest, was embroidering a fine handkerchief.

'... And that's how it is for young people, my poor Mademoiselle,' I heard Sofia Andreïevna say. 'You wait, you search, you get it wrong, you cry, you get over it... And what can you do to help them? All parents can do is pray to God.'

'God helps those who help themselves,' Mademoiselle said.

I slept with Nina that night. I was awoken by the sound of footsteps and doors slamming. I opened my eyes. It was barely light. I fell back asleep.

Very early the following day Nina and I had planned to build a hut out of branches at the back of the garden. We left the house bright and early without seeing anyone, bringing our lunch with us. As I was coming back, towards noon, happy and dishevelled, the first person I caught sight of was Mademoiselle.

'I've been looking for you everywhere,' she said. 'We're going home.'

'What? So early? Why?'

She didn't answer. She dragged me towards the hall. Through the open door I saw Sofia Andreïevna sitting in an armchair, her head thrown back, tears streaming down her pale, harrowed face, an unfolded letter on her lap. Then, all of a sudden, I heard Klavdia Alexandrovna's shrill laughter, grating and convulsive, ending in sobs and imprecations. Sofia Andreïevna had straightened herself up.

'Help! Help!' she cried frantically.

Mademoiselle, who always carried a little bottle of smelling salts with her—how many times had I found amusement in unscrewing the silver top and breathing in that sneeze-inducing scent?—rushed towards Klavdia and, naturally only too delighted by the occasion, I followed her.

Klavdia's arms were thrashing around in the air; the seizure wasn't feigned. At least I don't think so. She seemed to be suffocating.

'It's my fault! My fault!' she kept repeating. 'May God punish me!'

'What could you have done, my dear?' Sofia Andreïevna said to her, stroking her hair. 'If a mother didn't see or suspect anything, what could you have seen?'

'It's my fault, all my fault,' the other woman continued. 'It'll be the death of me.'

However, Mademoiselle, having made her breathe in the smelling salts, had stepped away from her and, standing by her side, was gazing coldly at her.

'I'm concerned for her…' Sofia Andreïevna said to Mademoiselle.

'If I were you,' she answered, 'I wouldn't worry.'

'Ah! it's just that she has such devotion, such a kind heart… This sorry situation will destroy her… and me,' she concluded in a broken voice.

I caught sight of Nina in the hall. She was gesturing to me through the half-open door. I joined her.

'What's going on?'

'I don't know,' she said very quietly, 'I don't understand. It seems Lola has run away with Uncle Serge. Maybe they'll get married. I don't understand why Mummy is crying. I'd be very happy.'

We discussed it for a moment and eventually found ourselves in agreement: Sofia Andreïevna was cross because it had all happened secretly, without her being consulted.

Then, since basically the whole story had nothing to do with us to the extent that we even felt embarrassed in a way, we took advantage of the confusion caused by the event to put our plan—long considered and continuously postponed—into action: to sneak into the kitchen and, in our own little way, make a few changes in there: to replace the salt with the sugar, to put the coal in the icebox and the cat with her kittens in the big pot.

'The cook will lift up the lid and the cats will jump up at her face. She'll put the fish in the ice and it'll come out all black. She'll think a spell's been put on her. She's always accusing Klavdia of witchcraft.'

This suddenly reminded me of the spell of fire, water and moonlight. I didn't say anything then, but a little later, in the tram that took me and Mademoiselle back home, I sidled up to her and whispered in her ear, 'I know why Klavdia Alexandrovna was in such a state.'

'Why?' Mademoiselle asked, probably too curious to think of answering me the way she usually did: Irène, you're poking your nose into grown-ups' business.

I told her the story of the magic game by the brook's edge, after the storm.

'Is it true, Mademoiselle? Did she really have a spell?'

'No, that's nonsense.'

'So why had Lola and Uncle Serge never thought of each other until then?'

'How do you know they never thought of each other in the first place?'

It was my turn to surprise her. I shrugged my shoulders with immense self-satisfaction.

'As if it's not obvious when someone's in love!'

Mademoiselle sighed and fell silent.

'It's obvious that she's behind it all,' I continued, flattered by her attention. 'And now she feels guilty because witchcraft is forbidden by God. So she's crying and repenting, and there you have it.'

Mademoiselle looked down at me with an expression I couldn't quite decipher, but which I didn't like: I hate when people are sarcastic with me, and besides, what did I say that was so funny?

'That must be it,' she said.

NATIVITY

At that time of year, in March, mild gusts, heavy with rain and salt, blew over the inland. The trees lining the road, tall dry poplars, in which crows' nests formed oakum knots, bent humbly under the force of the wind and straightened up with a reedy snigger; here and there little dark pools of water glittered faintly in the twilight. 'Miserable time of year to get engaged...' Yvonne sighed. She was in a hurry, twisting her high heels in the muck-filled ruts in the road. The sky was low and grey, the rain falling intermittently. The Armands' house in the Pas-de-Calais had been built eleven miles from the sea.

Yvonne came into the garden. At that time of year the first buds would usually be in bloom on the branches, but the winter had been long and harsh. The ground was black and waterlogged; only the old fir trees could grow freely, and the grass was grey and withered like hay. '*Ugly*,' muttered Yvonne, who was learning English in Saint-Omer. However, neither her parents nor her fiancé could speak any foreign language, so she sometimes talked to herself in English and in so doing felt a delicate, complex mix of pride in herself and a little contempt. In the house the maids were decorating the anteroom with potted azaleas and green plants. Madame Armand was rubbing wax polish into the staircase banister. Yvonne kissed her behind the ear, at the spot where her soft, wrinkled neck was marked by a deep furrow. Madame Armand had grey hair tied up in a bun on top of her head, dark eyes that had kept their sharpness, and a small mouth with thin, sunken lips. She rarely laughed, but her mouth creased at the corners in an expression that was impatient but tender, like the suppressed smile of someone speaking to noisy children. And so she let herself be kissed without saying a word, other than 'Isn't it about time you went and got dressed?'

But as her daughter climbed the stairs, Madame Armand sighed and her eyes followed her with an anxious, melancholic pride.

Yvonne entered her room, immediately closing the window, drew the curtains and smiled at the furniture lacquered in Trianon grey with a blue trim; her bedroom filled her heart with satisfaction. What's more, she would be taking everything with her. ('Papa has promised.') The walls were hung with pink and grey chintz; in the corners of the room were small tables so low that one had to hunker down on the carpet, on a cushion in order to write on them. 'You silly thing, what are you doing!' Brigitte had said. But Brigitte Carteret, Yvonne's older sister, had always adopted an amused, languorous inflection when speaking to her provincial family. She had always been strange and different from everyone else... Until that marriage that had caused her so much misery, Yvonne mused, picturing in her mind's eye her brother-in-law Antoine, his broad face, his dark eyes, the scornful little sneer on his beautiful lips. 'Antoine... is unpleasant,' she thought as she turned on the electric light housed in a porcelain flower, which stood atop the mirrored armoire. She took off her dress, put on a fresh slip and tied it over her shoulders in two pink ribbons. Yvonne was twenty years old. She was tall, stocky, vigorous, with an ample waist and breasts that were big for a girl of her age but very white and very firm. Her radiant blonde hair was cut short but was so fine and so full that one couldn't help but imagine it tied up in a big bun, as nature intended. She had a beautiful milky complexion, ruddy cheeks, a slightly broad nose and limpid grey eyes. She looked at herself with satisfaction; she was satisfied with herself and her life, and even more with her new dress lying on the bed: it was pink and fastened with a blue velvet belt knotted in a bow, which held a spray of artificial flowers. She finished dressing herself, carefully powdered her face and went downstairs.

Dinner had been arranged for seven o'clock. There was no great ceremony to it; only family and closest friends were to attend. Around the table decorated with flowers there were also a few girls sitting opposite other women: the fiancée, cousins withered already by their thirties and elderly women wearing mourning in memory of countless relatives. These young girls could foretell their own destinies, just as one might follow sheet music by singing quietly behind pursed lips, while at the piano another woman's triumphant voice rings out. Bouquets of white roses adorned the tablecloth, and behind each plate a rickety little salt cellar was nestled in a gap between the roses.

Yvonne's fiancé René Ponsard was sitting next to her; they didn't speak much but laughed nervously. Brigitte was sitting not far from her. 'She's changed so much lately!' Yvonne thought. She had indeed changed... Her pregnancies, the debts, the lawsuits and Antoine's mistresses—all that was enough to put years on anyone. She had three living children, three daughters, and now she was pregnant again. Every so often, like clockwork, she rearranged over her belly the folds of a fine lace jabot, which hid it a little. Then she turned her face away, gently tilting her head to one side. She had never looked like her sister Yvonne. She was short and waifish, with a fine-featured but ravaged face and greying locks, which she didn't dye but styled expertly; the mask of pregnancy had yellowed her features; the corners of her mouth, the wry, sensitive expression of which was truly beautiful, were marked by two tiny lines.

She only barely responded to those sitting around her, who were all cheer and chatter. Their broad faces, those of hearty eaters and drinkers and good hunters, were perched with great poise above their starched collars like calves' heads on white plates. Their eyes turned benevolently towards Yvonne and René and with pity towards Brigitte and Antoine. 'A lovely marriage, a marriage of inclination,' Madame Ponsard said softly. Yvonne heard her and smiled with confusion and delight... 'A marriage of inclination'... A lovely way of putting it... It was true that she had felt attracted to René from their first meeting. The engagement... doubtless a blissful time of enchantment: the trousseau, the gifts. Madame René Ponsard... She stole a tender glance at her fiancé.

They made a start on the ice cream, which was tall like a tower and decorated with spun sugar, nougat and glacé fruits.

Meanwhile, outside, night had fallen, a March night, damp and dark. The moon appeared in the stormy sky, lighting up the garage. The old women sighed.

A little later the guests left the table and took their seats in a circle in the drawing room. The girls began to dance to the sounds of the gramophone. Someone had put on an English record: *I'll be loving you always, always...*

'Schmaltzy doggerel, but the music is pretty,' Brigitte thought as she listened to the lively melody, which was full of sweet-sounding desperation. She folded her two translucent hands over her heavy belly. Antoine was standing behind her; she couldn't see him, but his presence bestowed on her a wonderful peace. She shivered, closed her eyes and opened them again with a slightly confused smile. 'This child is so painful to carry... Yvonne and René look like wax busts in a hairdresser's window display.' Her engagement, her own wedding hadn't looked like this... 'Even though I was born and bred in this house, between the linen armoire and the jam cupboard, I never had that saintly bisque face…' She repressed her irritation. 'Poor little Yvonne… Poor little porcelain doll…' She was twirling in her fiancé's arms and was humming: '*I'll be loving you always, always…*' Love… As if, with her rosy cheeks, that chest and her pale, empty eyes, she could ever know love… She remembered her first kiss. An autumn night, by the sea, among the sand dunes, beneath the violet sky. Antoine's warm lips… That devastating joy… The wind stirring the long grass among the dunes, drawing from the blades a plaintive cry. 'The poor thing is blind,' people said now. 'How can she not see he's being unfaithful to her? That he just gets money and pleasure out of her, without giving her anything in return…' She sighed. If her parents had known that since her last accident the doctors had told her not to get pregnant again… If they had known that between her youngest daughter and this one who was now stirring and kicking against the wall of her painful stomach ('Why are you in such a hurry?' she wondered. 'Do you think life's a walk in the park?'), yes, between those two, two other children had also longed to come into the world, but one was never to think of these things… Besides, what good would it do…? But at least she knew what love was, the bliss, the painful humility. 'But who here could ever understand me,' she thought with vanity. Only her father, with his plain-featured, melancholy face, seemed alive among these wax beings. But as he was her father, she turned her thoughts away from him with a sad indifference. She felt ill. Her pregnancies were difficult, this one particularly so. The suffocation she felt was worsened by the carefully closed windows—'They have such a fear of fresh air!'—and by the music. ('Dance, dance, little sister, your turn will come soon...') But of course it won't: Yvonne would say, 'René, darling, your mother says we mustn't have any more children, that it's more sensible,' and René would comply, 'take precautions' and make love to the factory girls.

She got up with some effort, leaning with both hands on the back of the armchair in front of her. Her hands were thin and white, adorned with a single band; her rings had long been sold. Antoine came up to her and opened the door for her; his manners were impeccable, she thought tenderly. He went out with her; when he touched her arm she once again felt a strange deep shiver; in her womb the child turned with an abrupt and painful jolt; when it fell back, it was as if her heart had stopped beating for a moment.

Antoine appeared nervous. He was biting his bottom lip irritably. He had probably tried once again, unsuccessfully, to borrow some money. And the child about to be born! In a flash she felt hopeless. Life was too sordid, too terrible, she thought, overwhelmed by it all. But Antoine was there... She took his hand, caressed it gently in the dark. The moon illuminated the gravel, the white pebbles glittering beneath their feet. The smell of earth and rain was rising from the narrow garden. Without saying a word, Antoine pressed her tightly against him; in this misshapen body, now heavier, he recognised a fierce and brave soulmate. He wasn't lying when he said,

'You're the only woman in my life, Brigitte…' He took her fine-featured, ravaged face in his hands, his warm palms gently cradling her cheeks. He looked deep into her fiery eyes, which were underlined with dark rings and lowered under his gaze. It was above all this painful humility that he enjoyed in her. He kissed her eyelids and then gently pushed her away. At that moment René and Yvonne emerged from the house; René was supporting his fiancée on his slightly plump arm, as if he were inviting her to dance a quadrille. She had thrown a woollen shawl over her pink dress. They slowly walked down the path to the half-open garage; the headlights of the parked car, illuminated by the moon, were glowing feebly in the dark like two big pale eyes. Yvonne tilted her head to one side. She and René were the same height, but she was stronger and more robustly built. He was weak and frail, with a pretty face, regular features, amber eyes, a fine golden moustache and small lips. His breathing sounded shallow and wheezing like that of a child obstructed by his tonsils, Yvonne thought all of a sudden. But she immediately chased these thoughts away, closed her eyes and waited. He took her in his arms; she felt his stiff shirtfront rub up against her face. He kissed her hair at random and her mouth clumsily. Then they drew apart from each other. He sighed softly, as if he felt the satisfaction of a job well done, and they went back in. The two mothers, standing behind the drawing room window, were breathing on the windowpanes and looking with both tenderness and concern at the bare, moonlit garden and the husband and wife-to-be, arm in arm. 'Aunt Marthe will give you a silver-gilt fish cutlery set, my dear children!' Madame Ponsard murmured to herself. Then she turned away and furtively dried her eyes. A little later ten o'clock chimed and the guests left.

Yvonne went back to her room and began to get ready to go to bed. Brigitte's bedroom was next to hers. She could hear her laboured breathing as she paced the room with a heavy, uniform step. One of the little girls, who slept on the other side of the corridor, cried faintly in the dark. Brigitte and Yvonne emerged from their rooms at the same time and entered the bedroom. Brigitte leant over the little beds. The children were asleep, radiant with beauty, their golden hair fanned out, their bare arms hanging out of the bedclothes. Beside them the mother seemed even paler and more exhausted. 'They're good children,' Yvonne said.

'The best,' Brigitte said mournfully, 'was the fourth, the one who wasn't born.'

Yvonne shuddered. Sometimes Brigitte's words sent a shiver of horror coursing through her veins. 'An older sister would have kissed me now,' Yvonne thought sadly, 'called me near her, shared my happiness. She's so strange!'

They parted. Back in her bedroom, between the grey furniture with the blue trim, with the electric radiator glowing, giving out a gentle heat, Yvonne felt at peace once again.

She lay down and clung to her pillow with both arms; it was soft and fresh; she yawned and closed her eyes. The wind blew through the open window and stirred the pink and grey chintz curtains, sending them billowing into the room to fall like two wings. She felt herself sinking, moving deeper towards dark, warm depths through which passed the faces of unknown men, where soft and strange voices rang out.

But it would all soon be over. It was only the troubled prelude to the peaceful, dreamless sleep that carried her each night to the following morning.

As she was falling asleep this way, she suddenly heard Brigitte crying out next door. She was up in an instant, her heart pounding, without understanding what was meant by this crying or the sound of footsteps through the sleeping house. A door slammed. She hurried through the moonlit corridor; Brigitte's door had remained ajar; she glimpsed Brigitte sitting up in her bed, panting, her back supported by cushions. Her face was white, and through her pursed lips could be heard a low, monotonous groan.

Antoine was standing by the window, smoking. Madame Armand was standing by the bed; her hair, plaited for the night, fell over her shoulders in two meagre grey braids. She turned around promptly.

'Go away!…' she said in a hushed voice, recognising Yvonne. 'You shouldn't be here…'

'Is the child about to be born?' Yvonne murmured.

Her mother bowed her head. Yvonne noticed that the old hands holding Brigitte's wrists were trembling slightly. At that moment Brigitte's face convulsed; from her open mouth came a scream, twisted, it seemed, by the violence of the pain. Yvonne fled. She realised that she had passed by her bedroom, that she was going down to the kitchen. In that cold room the flowers had been put in big jugs for the night. They exuded a heady scent. The two maids were up, hastily dressed, their bare feet peeping out from underneath their smocks. They had lit the gas and were heating the water while talking quietly among themselves and yawning with sleepy, sullen expressions. Yvonne looked at them for a moment, then she felt the cold of the tiles chilling her feet through her flimsy slippers. She felt embarrassed by her disarray, by her presence in the kitchen and by the maids' curious gazes. Through the misted up windowpanes she saw her father taking the car out of the garage.

'Monsieur is going to get the doctor,' the short maid said indifferently.

The gas whistled and the water boiled over. A muffled cry rang out through the house. All three of them looked up at the same time and, their faces turning pale, they waited.

'Mother of God!' the cook said softly.

Yvonne left the kitchen. Behind her the silence returned.

'Of course,' she heard the maid murmur, 'when Alida gave birth last year...'

She lowered her voice and whispered rapidly for a moment. Yvonne slowly went back upstairs. She had left her bedroom door ajar; she sat down on the edge of the bed, leaning forward, listening to those cries piercing through her ears, like the fearsome words of an unknown language that she might have tried to make sense of, but to no avail. ('And what about me... One day?...')

'No!' she thought, recalling with indignation Antoine's calm face. 'It will be different for me!…'

She closed her eyes, forced herself to imagine the church, the white satin dress, the long train, the veil, the flowers, René leaning towards her, kissing her mouth; then later, beautiful, clean children with curly hair, dressed in white…

Yes, but those too will be born among these cries, that pain, that confusion… '*Ugly, ugly!*' she murmured automatically with a sudden shiver. Listening carefully, between the screams, Yvonne could hear the creaking of the old bed on which Brigitte was stretched out. Yvonne threw herself forward, burying her head in the cushions, but the moaning and that strange panting she could hear didn't cease. She turned the light off, but the moonlight slipping through the bare branches terrified her.

Again she arose abruptly, closed the shutters and the window, drew both the little tulle curtains and the heavier curtains and pinned them together so that no night-time light or sound of the wind could come through; in the lamplight she looked at the porcelain animals, the little shelves, the Christmas roses in the vases, seeking to forget what was coming to pass near her.

Brigitte had suddenly fallen quiet. The silence was so deep that Yvonne fell half asleep, sinking into a kind of troubled torpor.

An hour passed in this way. All of a sudden a louder cry woke her with a start. She sat up on the bed, her heart pounding.

A torn body, probably, the blood gushing out of it…

166

The gloomy, terrifying image filled her with fear and shame.

At that very moment she heard hurried steps running along the corridor; her mother was passing by her door. 'Mother!' she called, and she was taken aback by the violence of the cry that came out of her.

Her mother came in, looked at her with turmoil in her eyes and then made a visible effort to calm down.

'Well? Have you gone mad, shouting like that?...' she whispered automatically. 'Things... are going according to plan. The doctor's coming...'

Her lips stiffened imperceptibly.

'She doesn't want me to stay with her,' her mother continued. 'She wants to be alone with her husband.'

Yvonne went back to bed. Her mother stayed standing with her ear pressed against the door, her whole body leant forward, ready to run to Brigitte at the slightest call, but the only words discernible from the cries and the confused moaning were 'Antoine!... Antoine!...' Then only the tireless cries could be heard filling the house. They followed a strange rhythmic pattern: they rose in measured waves, dying down and swelling up again with a kind of soothing, solemn cadence. Yvonne stole a glance at her mother.

Her old body was trembling, contracting painfully, as if it remembered, as if after all those years it recognised the rhythm and the very pain of childbirth. 'Soon,' Madame Armand thought, 'soon it will be Yvonne's turn...' The two names echoed within her like an antiphony: 'Brigitte... Yvonne...' Her heart bled for both of them.

It… the child… was nothing yet… A few hours of suffering, very soon over, very soon forgotten… but the rest, one's whole life… love… She had guessed, through Brigitte's reticence, her sighs, that by accepting this child she was putting her own life at risk… 'But they're all the same,' she thought. 'Do they ever consider the suffering they put me through?'

'If only I'd known…' she said restlessly, looking at Yvonne, 'I would never have left you here. A young girl… But who could have predicted an accident?'

She fell silent upon seeing the lamps being turned on downstairs. The doctor was coming up the stairs. She rushed after him. Yvonne saw her father pause before the closed door, bury his head in his hands and slowly go back downstairs. She was alone again.

Little by little the cries subsided and turned into a strange, monotonous groaning. The smell of chloroform was coming through the walls. The groaning itself then ceased.

A heavy silence fell once again. Outside the rain had stopped. Only the leaves stirred now and then under the force of the wind, sending waterdrops hurtling towards the ground. She heard the maids coming up the stairs; they were careful not to make too much noise with their footsteps; they paused in the corridor, outside Yvonne's half-open door. She heard their sighs and the heavy step of their soles coming down carefully on the old creaking floorboards. Someone called out quietly; someone on the stairs seemed to be carefully carrying a heavy object; Yvonne suddenly heard it rolling down the corridor, together with the sound of rustling straw and wrapping paper. Yvonne recognised it as being the old cradle from the attic, which had been taken down in a hurry, bare, still wrapped in straw and canvas. Then the intermittent whispering started up again, but little by little the tired women became quiet and the deep, heavy silence fell once again.

'Brigitte's going to die,' Yvonne thought. She closed her eyes wearily. One was not to think of such things. Her dresses, the trousseau, the ceremony, Aunt Marthe's gift, Aunt Cécile's gift... Aunt Cécile was dying of cancer... But one was not to think of such things... Aunt Cécile was dying... she would inherit... that wasn't called cancer, suffering, death, but inheritance, hope... Twelve small silver-gilt spoons... the wedding-march, the big red carpet... Yes, but what did it lead to? No doubt to the altar. And then?... To dark, unknown, frightening joys, then to a painful birth like this one... then to old age and death...

Someone was walking over the gravel beneath her window. She recognised the footsteps as being Antoine's. René would be different. René would be loving and tender... She saw once again in her mind's eye René's sharp, fine-featured face. 'He has the profile of a fox...' she thought with unease. 'I've never noticed before...' That sunken lip and those copper eyes, affectionate, deceitful... She shook her head. No, no, one was not to think of that either... She must have been falling half-asleep, and as happens in half-sleep, the closest, the most familiar images take on a strange and terrifying form… One had to sleep, sleep… Like long ago, in her childhood, when she recited fables to herself to bring on sleep, she began to hum quietly: *I'll be loving you always, always… With a love that's true… always, always…* She started suddenly. A little cry, a shrill mew had rung out in the silence. The piercing, weak, miserable cry of a little child… Was it alive then? 'Is it another daughter?' she thought. 'I will have sons…'

Madame Armand appeared on the threshold. She had pinned up her grey plaits. Her face was pale and exhausted, her eyes red.

'Another daughter,' she said quietly, 'and alive… At seven months, it's a miracle… But Brigitte…'

She paused and absent-mindedly made Yvonne's bed, pulling the sheets with her old skilful hands, which were nonetheless trembling imperceptibly.

'Sleep. Why aren't you sleeping? Did you really have to listen?' she said in a weary and reproachful voice.

'How is Brigitte, Mother?' Yvonne murmured with fear in her voice.

'She's very weak, the poor thing,' the mother said, turning her face away, 'but we must have hope. Sleep, my little one, sleep,' she continued in an unusually tender tone, lightly stroking Yvonne's forehead. 'Sleep.'

She left the room. Yvonne remained motionless for some time. She then gently pushed away the bedclothes and got up.

'I'd like to see Brigitte,' she thought, trembling. 'And the child… It's horrid, sordid,' she thought, with a feeling of fright and shame, 'but the very fear of it draws you in…'

She listened for a moment at the bedroom door, which was firmly shut. Inside it was silent. Holding her breath, she pushed the double door open and went in. A nurse, a big tall woman with an ample chest compressed under her white coat and canvas apron, was lying asleep in an armchair. Some coffee was being heated on a lit bedside stove. The flames were still glowing in the fireplace; the logs were stacked precariously; they crackled and split down the middle, revealing the pink and black heart of the flames. The embers in turn collapsed with a soft whistle. 'She's so quiet,' Yvonne thought. She let her gaze pour over the bed, but Brigitte's stillness frightened her: 'She's not dead, though. The child wouldn't have been left here…' She approached the cradle. Bare as it was, without any ribbons or mousseline, the old yellowed wicker shell was a heart-rending sight. She leaned forward slightly and shuddered with disgust on seeing the child, who looked more like an amputated limb, still bleeding and throbbing, than a human being. Its scalp was soft and bald. It had neither eyelashes nor nails. It was the first newborn she'd ever seen. She had imagined only chubby pink children like the angels painted on boxes of dragées. It was asleep. It seemed crushed with exhaustion. She stepped away from the cradle, made two steps towards Brigitte's bed and paused again. The nurse, now awake, looked at her with an air of surprise and hostility… The child began to squirm and cried feebly. The nurse rocked the cradle with a yawn, looked at her and shook her head.

'She must be allowed to rest, Mademoiselle. I'll call you if things take a turn for the worse.'

'She's not going to die, is she?' Yvonne murmured.

'We can't say for the moment,' the nurse said evasively.

She took Brigitte's hand, felt her pulse for a moment, tapped her wrist indifferently and let it fall again.

'You can come closer if you like…' she said.

Yvonne hesitated.

'There's nothing to be frightened of…' the nurse said quietly. 'She's weak and she's lost a lot of blood, but I've seen others come through worse… You can kiss her if you like, Mademoiselle,' she added after a moment's reflection, 'but then go… It's not light yet…'

Yvonne leaned towards the pale still face and looked at it ardently. Brigitte seemed to be sleeping; her breathing was light. Her features were stiff and still. Yvonne realised with a start that her eyes were wide open and fixed on some invisible point; her eyebrows were raised in an anxious, weary expression, like someone gazing out towards the sea in search of a boat or just some light walnut shell carried away by the current. Her hands fell back on either side of her body, open feebly, the palms pallid and translucent, emptied of their blood. Overwhelmed by a strange serenity, Yvonne looked at her for some time. 'Poor Brigitte… But no,' she thought, 'why? Even if she has to die… she doesn't seem unhappy. She's calm… she no longer has that expression of painful sarcasm and worry… Why?' she thought, contemplating that severe, calm face that was peacefully falling asleep…

She gently pressed her lips against Brigitte's thin cheek, where a shadowed hollow was forming under her prominent cheekbone. She straightened herself up. The nurse, now sitting under the lamp, was knitting rapidly. The child was sleeping without a sound. She left the room.

Back in her own room, she paused in the middle of it and, with a gesture that came as some surprise to her, for it was not a habit of hers, she rubbed her hand over her forehead for a long time, as if searching for a fleeting thought. And suddenly it came back to her: 'My engagement night…' she thought with dismay. That night… which she had imagined to be so beautiful, so poetic… ending like this in such a sordid and ugly way! She felt tears of irritation swelling in her eyes… From the very beginning everything had been so different from what she had imagined… Even this dark and rainy March day. She approached the window automatically, opened the blinds and paused suddenly with surprise. Day was breaking and the wind had turned. Stretching her face outside, she felt that even the taste of the air had changed during the night. The west wind, the wind blowing from the sea, had carried with it that soft, fertile rain and the gentle, fragrant breath of spring. On the damp black earth the pools of water sparkled, reflecting the first rays of sunshine. Over the horizon a dense fog still covered the Bois de la Houlette; the mist was clearing over the lawn, leaving big glittering water-drops behind. A warm, impatient wind stirred the branches, from which the rain fell suddenly with a light and lively sound; the first cocks had long crowed hoarsely in the fog; others, closer by, were now crowing; the carts could be heard creaking along the road. The sun had risen.

Yvonne remained still; a feeling of peace, of contentment, for which there was no explanation, engulfed her. For the first time in her life she stayed still, without thinking, her eyes closed, breathing in slowly the pure, gentle air of the first days of spring. Now and then it seemed to her that her soul was strained by a kind of anxiousness, a kind of desire, but that a sense of relief, a profound satisfaction, then immediately permeated her. She was breathing more fully now, more calmly. Everything around her seemed permeated by the same peace; the slightest sounds, the quivering of the grass, the faint rumble of the wind over the meadow behind the house—she could hear the wind rising, swelling, rushing and disappearing towards the Bois de Berre—a light whistling from the stirring leaves, the cocks' distant crowing, the little factory bell ringing out quietly in the idle silence, everything seemed so perfectly in its place, so necessary, as if there was a strict but tranquil order. A kind of anxious pang of unfulfilled desire that she had always harboured, but whose presence she had until now never recognised, was rising up, tensing, longing to be answered, to be appeased. This peace in her heart she could not yet sense, but for the first time in her life she could feel that expectation of, that hope for a mysterious bliss. And never again in her placid existence, which would pass in whole without any great joy or pain, would she be as close to it. But little by little this strange contentment dissipated. Like when the scattered notes of a symphony to an unmusical ear seem to gather around a central theme, when it seems that some harmony finally reached will fill the soul with a peaceful and eternal joy, everything falls apart senselessly, disintegrates, fades away and dies.

She turned aside, closed the window again and drew away from it. She suddenly felt at once irritated and weary. Brigitte... the child... How annoying!... 'As long as she doesn't die... If she dies, the wedding will have to take place in the strictest privacy,' she thought involuntarily. But she chased away that useless, gloomy thought immediately. Brigitte would get better. Hadn't the nurse said 'I've seen others come through worse...'? The three little girls would carry the long white satin train. The bridesmaids would carry round bouquets of tightly bound short-stemmed flowers wrapped in pleated paper like an Elizabethan collar, with edges pinked like lace, and blue aumônières embroidered in the traditional way, with silver florets... Six bridesmaids dressed in blue... No men among the attendants: they were coarse and clumsy... In her imagination René himself assumed the indistinct form of a dream. He was nothing but the husband now, a ceremonial character, all dressed up, perfumed, his face pomaded, with a white boutonnière in his lapel, a smile on his lips... She suddenly recalled Antoine and Brigitte on their wedding day, so beautiful, so tenderly united. A strange little snigger escaped from her lips. It surprised her. 'I'm so nervous...' she mumbled with unease. Despite herself, she kept turning towards the wall, imagining in the neighbouring room the pale, weary woman, the child whining in its cradle. 'Poor little thing,' she sighed. The silence was broken by the sound of the door opening. The nurse was leaving the bedroom, finding her way with a heavy step towards the stairs, her broad hips swinging from side to side.

Yvonne walked to the threshold and looked at her questioningly.

'Still the same… There's no danger for the time being. I'm going downstairs to get some water. I'll only be gone a minute. You can stay with her for a while if you like,' the woman said.

Yvonne hesitated, then went back into her room, rummaged around in the dressing table drawer for a moment and eventually took out a little flat packet wrapped in tissue paper. Carefully, holding her breath, she entered her sister's bedroom. This time, however, she didn't look at anything, neither the fire, which had died down again, nor Brigitte, stretched out, motionless in the shadow. She didn't even look at the child lying deep in the cradle like someone shipwrecked on a beach, surrounded, half-submerged by the dark waves of death, struggling bravely against them with all the strength of her feeble limbs. Yvonne looked away timorously, and in that bare bedroom where a woman's life was silently coming to an end and a child had just been born, in order to cover the starkness of the undressed cradle, to disguise its icy beauty, as if duty-bound, hurriedly and with unsteady, trembling hands, she tied to its iron handle a broad pink ribbon.